ELORA'S SONG

THE CARAGH CHRONICLES # 2

RACHEL A. JAMES

Edited by: Julie Cosgrove

Cover and Map Design: Rossano Designs

For more information on Rachel A. James please visit her website:

www.rachelajames.com

THE CARAGH CHRONICLES
SERIES BOOKS

Riona's Promise - Rachel Skatvold (Book 1)

Elora's Song - Rachel A. James (Book 2)

Cinnia's Fortune - Rachel Rossano (Book 3)

Land of Caragh

Chapter One

"They're arriving." Aimee squealed with delight as she fanned her face in exaggerated emphasis, as was her way. "Come and see. So many handsome knights, all staying at Carisleau for an entire week!"

Elora quirked her brow as she concentrated on the braid instead of the window. "Are their faces not concealed by their helmets?"

"You know what I mean."

Elora chose not to argue with her cousin, for Aimee's young heart held good intent. And as she was by far the most beautiful woman in the area, the tournaments and accompanying banquets would be a wonderful opportunity for her to meet new suitors. Indeed, the chance for an excellent match fared well. Elora hoped her cousin would find a man of kind character, not one of those peacocks that strutted their way inside the walls.

The tournaments had started out as military training opportunities during times of peace, but they had become more elaborate and competitive over time. Ladies traveled far to spectate in the grandeur, hoping to be swooped off their feet by a strong, handsome stranger who represented the ideals of chivalry, honor, and nobility. However, in her experience, Elora feared such qualities were rare indeed.

"There, your hair is beautiful, Cousin. Now I must bid my leave and tend Aunt Beatrice."

"Must you go? I have not yet chosen a gown, and you are far more apt at selecting just the perfect dress."

"My dear, we've maids for a reason. I will send for Clarice—"

"Lorie, please?" Aimee stuck out her bottom lip as she scrunched her eyebrows together.

Elora burst into laughter. She never could resist it when her younger cousin used the name of her childhood. "Very well. Let's see... how about your blue velvet?"

"Splendid. Will you help lace the sleeves?"

Elora nodded. She lifted the robe over Aimee's head, attached the arms, and fiddled with the revealing parts of the chemise until it appeared just right. Then she turned Aimee toward the looking glass and sighed. "They'll be writing songs about your beauty, and such knowledge will spread to the ends of the kingdom."

Aimee giggled. "You are such a tease."

Elora pinched Aimee's cheeks. "I mean every word. Now, I really must be off. I am not even dressed myself, and..."

Before she could complete her sentence, Aimee sprinted down the hallway in a most unladylike manner, no doubt in pursuit of her knights of valor.

Elora sighed and headed down the corridor toward her Aunt Beatrice's chamber. The curtains hung heavily, blocking out the daylight or any chance of a summer breeze. With a sharp intake of breath, she knocked on the open door before entering. "Is there anything you need, Aunt?"

Beatrice angled her head upwards, her wrinkled brow confirming Elora's suspicions.

"Do you have another headache?"

Her aunt grimaced but held up her hand upon Elora's approach. "There's no need to fuss, for naught can be done."

"I can fetch you a remedy from Gias—"

"Elora, I've been drinking your concoctions for years and they do little to alleviate my pain. No, all I need is slumber. 'Tis the stress of this tournament, I've no doubt. For when will another opportunity arise to find Aimee a suitor? Little happens in this part of the kingdom. We scarcely have visitors." She glanced up at Elora and drew in a breath. "Gracious, child, you cannot intend to greet our guests looking as you do. You must change immediately."

Elora cast a self-conscious glance over her simple gray woolen dress. Heat rose to her cheeks. "I have been too busy to ready myself, but I fully intend to before this evening's banquet."

Her aunt tutted. "No, child, you will do so now, for I cannot greet our guests this day. I must rest if I am to attend tonight's festivities."

"Aimee is ready, I am sure she and Uncle can—"

"What a thought." The shock laced in her aunt's voice did not go amiss. "Aimee is a thousand times more beautiful than you will ever be but let us not pretend she has any degree of sense or propriety. She will surely scare off any suitors the moment she opens her mouth. No, this must be planned with care. You will welcome them and put them at ease. Then, when they are relaxed with merriment, we'll introduce Aimee into society."

"She is not an embarrassment, Aunt, mayhap a little youthful—"

At her aunt's stern face, Elora knew not to push the subject. "But I'll of course, see to our guests. I will check on you a little later." She kissed her aunt's forehead and closed the chamber door behind her. Taking a moment to exhale, she expelled any troubling emotions that threatened the pit of her stomach and sent up a quick prayer for Aunt Beatrice. Then she picked up her pace to find her uncle in the library, hiding away from the noise and commotion of all that a busy residence entailed.

"Close the door."

Elora padded through the vast chamber, running her fingers along the books as she neared her uncle. She could understand why Uncle Reginald sought seclusion here. Even though his failing eyes now prevented him from reading, the scent of manuscripts alone must bring him familiarity and comfort. She considered this one of the few peaceful places left in Carisleau.

She leaned over her uncle's shoulders and rested her chin on his head. "The guests are here."

He turned toward her. "I thought as much. Have you checked on your aunt? I fear she has come down with one of her headaches again."

"Yes, I will see to today's demands so she can stay in her chamber until the banquet."

"I suppose Aimee's found the knights' encampment?"

Elora grinned. "You know her too well. It will take all of heaven and earth to keep her away from them at this hour."

"Then I am sorry for this all to fall on you, my dear. Will you take me to them?"

She hesitated, casting a glance over her simple day dress. "Yes Uncle, but Aunt says I must first change—"

"I am sure you're fine, dear. You've ample time to prepare before the banquet. Now, I hear the arrival of our guests, and there is someone I would like you to meet."

Elora's clothing was the least of her worries. She should be more concerned about the mess of her long hair, not having had a chance to pin it up, as protocol dictated. Oh, how she missed the simplicity of being a novice nun. A quick glance at her fingernails, and she hid her hands within her sleeves. She needed a bath, and a few moments of solitude herself.

Lord Reginald rose, his shoulders rounded from years spent stooping over manuscripts and paperwork. He squeezed her chin fondly. "I am glad you chose not the convent. Their loss is indeed our gain."

A pang of guilt stabbed her heart at the reminder of her desertion. Sighing, she took his arm in hers and escorted him out of the library and toward the party of finely dressed men getting down from their horses.

"Ah, I would recognize that voice anywhere." Uncle's tone brightened. "Sir Gerard, 'tis an honor for you to stay with us. We have prepared the finest of chambers for you and your men. This is my niece, Lady Elora, and she will ensure your care. My daughter, is..." He waved his hand warily. "Somewhere, and is very excited to meet you as well."

Elora caught her breath in her throat, sure her heart stopped beating at the very sound of his name. Recognition flashed briefly across his face before he bowed his head, took her hand in his and kissed it. "Lady Elora, a pleasure."

Her skin numbed at his touch. How long had it been? Five years? His features were more refined than her recollection of him. A slight scar on the side of his chin, barely noticeable beneath his carefully trimmed beard, only deepened his ruggedly handsome appearance. God help her.

"Sir Gerard lived here many years ago. You were at the convent during his time here as a squire."

Her uncle had been in Morgandy with Aimee during their previous meeting that summer. He never knew... She sucked in a breath. "Greetings, Sir. And from where do you hail now?"

"I've just returned from the king's campaigns. His Lordship invited me here for the week."

Elora wrinkled her brow. "As part of the garrison?" She never would have pictured him...

"No, my lady, I—"

Lord Reginald cleared his throat. "As our esteemed troubadour. Have you not heard of the great Gerard de Castille?

After his service here, he studied music with the famous Master Jacques Lonrique."

"M-music?" After all this time, he'd become a troubadour? A serious musician and composer. Had Gerard's aspirations truly come to fruition?

She swallowed, suddenly feeling lightheaded. "Please excuse me, I have much to attend to."

Feeling a flush rise in her cheeks, she dared not look at them and departed for her chamber. Her uncle would have to show the knights to their quarters, for she did indeed need to ready herself. Now, more than ever.

Once inside the safety of her room, she leaned against the door and stared idly at her writing table. She must off-load or this would drive her mad. Taking a fresh quill and parchment, Elora sat down to pen a letter to her friend.

Dearest Riona,

I was hoping to see you at the tournament this week, but I warrant you must be busy. I confess, there is a reason for this letter. You may remember that when I wrote to you some years ago, the summer that I returned to Carisleau Castle, I met a handsome squire and fell in love. We were both so young, and I believed a calling for the order, and he wished to study music and become a composer. I refused his proposal based on our different paths.

You will be shocked to learn, however, that today I encountered him again, and my feelings have quite unexpectedly resurfaced. Did I do the right thing by refusing him? He is now the great Sir Gerard de Castille, a renowned knight and troubadour, and I...? My double mindedness is my undoing! There are moments when I miss the nunnery terribly, but then I see Gerard and my heart longs for him like naught I've ever known! How can this be?

Please advise me, for I have always welcomed your wise counsel on such matters.

Your dearest friend,
Elora

Writing about her anxieties seemed to ease her concerns. Her time at the convent, where she'd received her education from the nuns at Sisters of Mercy, had been some of the happiest moments of her life and she'd formed lifelong friendships. Progression into the nunnery as a novice had been the natural next step, only...

Should she have accepted Gerard's proposal, despite being so young and naïve? Sighing, she slid off her woolen day dress, stared in the mirror and examined the faint dark circles around her eyes with a trembling hand.

"Need some help, m'lady?"

Elora blinked, taking a moment to focus on her maid's reflection in the glass. "Clarice, I did not hear you come in." She held a quivering hand to her chest, her heart beating worryingly fast.

"Are you well? You look like you've seen a ghost."

Elora returned her gaze to the mirror. "It is a strange notion to look at one's reflection and no longer see the youthful image that once was."

"Is that what worries you so? I expect the tournament has you in a flurry of nerves. All these gallant knights roaming the castle. Would you like me to give you a hand in your preparations?"

She shook her head. "No indeed. I thought you were taking food to your family in the village."

"I'll go by later. There is so much going on this day, you could use the extra help."

"I cannot argue with that." Elora released a small chuckle. "I'm afraid my nerves threaten to best me, and my hand will not stop shaking."

Clarice smiled. "Then let me fix that hair of yours. We'll have you looking like a princess in no time."

Gerard's mouth turned dry. Why was Elora here, and not dressed in habit? She avoided eye contact with him as her cheeks flushed rose-pink. Elora shifted her feet and made her excuses to leave, only for him to realize he'd barely spoken a word to her. But bombarding her with questions in front of her uncle and his men was not wise, either. God had spared him that embarrassment, he supposed.

"Forgive my niece," apologized Lord Reginald. "She has much to do, as you can imagine. We rely on her greatly to see to the running of the household. My wife is often taken to her bed with sickness, you see."

"I thought your niece had decided on a life at the convent, my lord. Does not Lady Aimee..."

He knew Aimee would be an unlikely person to rely upon to help Lady Beatrice, but there was no other way to enquire of Elora without it looking suspicious.

"No, no, Elora is much needed here, and thank God she chose this duty rather than the nunnery. I am near useless now, with my failing eyesight the way it is. And with Lady Beatrice's episodes..." Reginald paused—his face suddenly raw with emotion.

The poor man, he was a fraction of the mighty baron that Gerard remembered. As if hearing Gerard's thoughts, Reginald straightened and forced a smile. "But we are much glad you visit us, Sir. I hope you are ready to perform and cheer us all this week."

"Indeed, I am, my lord. Allow me to introduce my fellow men." He gestured toward the entourage behind him, and then slapped Owain's shoulder. "This is my good friend, Sir Owain. He competes in the tournament."

Reginald gripped Owain's hand and shook it firmly. "Welcome to Carisleau. Come, you will wish to ready yourselves for this eventide, I trust. We have prepared the finest of our rooms for you."

They followed the old man as he ambled adequately along the corridor, and despite his apparent poor eyesight, clearly knew the way around the castle.

"What has gotten into you?" growled Owain, as they followed Reginald through the Great Hall.

"You did not notice the lady who greeted us?"

"What about her? Why should you concern yourself with..." Owain pulled a face. "Ah. She is Lorie? Your childhood beau?"

Gerard swallowed. "Hardly a child... she was sixteen when I met her."

Owain exhaled a whistle. "Brother, what pain you must endure! You left Carisleau because you could not deal with your beloved taking the vow. Then, to disappear for half a decade, only to discover she never became one?" He halted and turned to face Gerard. "I wonder why she did not marry. Mayhap she's been waiting for you all this time. Now is your opportunity!"

"She rejected me once. I'll not face such humiliation again."

Owain eyed him then shrugged as they resumed their way down the hall. "Well, you're to perform soon. Better compose yourself."

"There is naught to compose, other than my music, of course. I loved her, yes, but that was a long time ago. I laid aside any of my feelings for her the day I left this castle."

"And now you're returned?" Owain gave a lopsided grin.

"I am at peace with the decision we made. Do not fear for me, my good friend. I shall be perfectly able to conduct myself in a goodly manner."

They soon entered the south wing of the castle, where a warm fire crackled beneath an enormous hearth.

Reginald hovered at the door and motioned them inside. "I trust you will be comfortable here. There are extra beds for your men, as you can see."

Gerard thanked their host and settled himself down on the chair by the fire. He pulled out his lute. His fingers played the tune his mind always drew to when melancholy and loss permeated his soul.

"Come, man. Play something cheery. You'll send us all to an early grave with a song like that."

Gerard eyed Owain's intense stare. "Fair enough." He slung the instrument aside and instead picked up his vielle. With gusto, he played something from his former days, before the war across the seas, when love was a joy and not a burden to his heart.

Then he rose and stared into the flames. "I did the right thing? Coming home?"

Owain pulled a face. "You feel guilty for abandoning the king's campaign."

He sighed. "'Tis a possibility. Carisleau has a chest full of memories."

Owain's squire, Ambrose, snorted. "You're worried you'll have naught but love to write about now that the campaigns are over."

His men broke into laughter.

"Mayhap I'll write a song about you, Ambrose."

"Be sure to mention his most fortunate success with women." Owain winked.

Ambrose crossed his arms. "That was just one time. I knew not she was betrothed. Besides, I only talked to her. What is so wrong with that?"

Gerard recalled the incident in the tavern. "Her beau certainly had something to say on the matter."

"Say? He gave me a broken nose."

Owain roared once more. "He did you a favor, enhanced your looks no end. The ladies like a war scar."

"I hardly think that counts as a battle wound. Besides, my nose is not improved." He held up a blade and stared at his reflection. "If you peruse it from this angle, it's as crooked as the beams in your house, Owain."

Gerard sat between the two of them to avoid any further banter. It would not take much for this to turn into a brawl.

"Come now, we must prepare for tonight's feast. I hear there are plenty of ladies in attendance…" He slapped his own face as if preparing for a fight, then headed for the hall to practice. There was no place for error this evening.

Clarice stilled at the gathering of the local villagers in her family's home. She eyed her father, Maxim, as she slipped inside, careful not to disrupt whatever business they conducted. He glanced up momentarily but paid her little heed.

"Our children are starving." His voice sounded gruff and animated. "We've no time to farm our own crops because we're so busy tending old Reginald's, and now with increased taxes…"

Murmurs of agreement filtered through the room.

Clarice sucked in a breath at the disgruntled folk. She was fortunate to have employment at the castle, but her family did not share such security. She passed the leftover bread that her mistress had given her round the overly crowded room.

Her father took a piece and waved it at his friends. "There is talk of an uprising. A clan from Morgandy plans to attack Carisleau and they are looking for supporters."

"But Dada, you are loyal to Lord Reginald. To say such things is treachery—"

Clarice's father glared at her interruption. She'd not planned to make a scene in his home. Even so, if she became affiliated with a rebellion her job would be at risk.

"Your daughter is right, Maxim. We've benefitted from your Clarice's position. To join this uprising would endanger our families."

"I do not wish to go against our lord, Severin, but what can be done? You said so yourself, you'd not be able to pay your taxes this quarter. Why is it your fault that your ox died? How are you supposed to afford another animal? How will you feed your children this winter? Here we toil and suffer, whilst the nobles have so much food, they can hold a week-long banquet? Mayhap, to instill change, treachery must be at play."

Clarice could not believe what she was hearing. "There has to be another way. Lord Reginald is a kind and generous master. I am sure if you talk to him—"

Their laughter sent the hairs on the back of Clarice's arms to stand.

"The time for talking has passed. There is a knight, known only to the people as 'The Gray', who has been touring the circuit. There are rumors that he is the lost King of Edan."

Clarice gasped under her breath, but this time chose not to challenge her father.

"I too have heard these rumors, but what of them, Maxim?"

"If captured, we can claim a king's ransom. If he is not the king, naught is lost. But if he is, then our reward is the reform that we seek."

Clarice chewed her fingernails, sweat forming on her brow. To be witness to such treason, and to be associated with such perpetrators, put her in an impossible situation. But what could be done? She was a mere servant girl.

Chapter Two

Elora remained motionless. Time stilled. Goosebumps formed on her arms at the richness of Gerard's voice as he sang with breathtaking conviction. She swiped at a tear before anyone could notice.

Aimee leaned closer to whisper in Elora's ear. "I must say, Gerard is quite remarkable. His songs are so raw and haunting, do you not think?"

"Yes, I wonder what he must have endured in battle, what horrors he surely witnessed to inspire such heart-rendering emotion."

"I do think he is much changed. Of course, it's doubtful you will even remember him, having spent so much time at the abbey."

Elora closed her eyes. Her mind flashed back to the summer she met Gerard. He had danced with her, much like those around her were beginning to do now. She had rejected him, and yet he was now the epitome of the ideal suitor.

Gerard finished his performance, and the minstrels continued to play. Elora did not wish to collide paths with him so soon. "Do you think anyone will notice if I slip out?"

Aimee opened her mouth to protest, but then became suitably distracted by Sir Owain's approach toward her.

Seizing the opportunity, Elora eased her way out of the room. She intended to go to the library, but her feet took her southward and she soon found herself in the chapel. Mayhap her heart knew best. This room always reminded her of her days in the convent. Surrounded by either peaceful silence or tranquil music, calming faith reigned in her heart. Each time she chanted with the nuns, those sacred words brought her such comfort. She'd sung them so often; she need not see the manuscripts to recite them by heart. Amidst the stillness, she sung them quietly to herself once again.

> *The Lord is my comfort and keeper*
> *His strength, a pillar, Hallelujah.*
> *My soul singeth his praises.*
> *His presence within me dwelleth.*
> *I shall not fear the adversary*
> *Nor be part of the devil's schemes.*
> *For my God is victorious in all things.*

As the song echoed around the chapel walls, the familiar melody returned to her ears. Life had been simple in the nunnery. She'd existed only to serve God and her community, but society for a noble young woman had become far more complicated than living within the safety of Sisters of Mercy. She swiped at the tears on her cheek and turned to leave.

In the doorway stood Gerard, and Elora froze at the sight of him.

"Sir—Sir Gerard I—"

Footsteps sounded down the corridor. "There you are, man. We've been challenged to a game of water shields. Care to join?"

Gerard nodded without breaking eye contact with her until he finally turned on his heels.

Elora barely had time to exhale before Aimee sped round the corner, her slippers skidding on the stone floor. She entered, her face filled with profound excitement. "We're going to the lake. Come, you should accompany me."

"At this time of night? It is most improper."

"Which is why you must come, silly cousin. You can chaperone."

Elora swallowed. "Pardon me?"

Aimee grabbed her arm, dragging her out of the chapel. "Make haste."

"Oh, very well."

Once Aimee had her heart set on something, there would be no reasoning with her. Besides, Aimee was young. Of course she wanted fun. As they reached the lake, knights were already half clothed and swinging from the tree into the water.

Elora tightened her grip on Aimee's arm. "Take heed to preserve your dignity, Cousin."

Aimee rolled her eyes and tucked her skirt into her girdle, and then followed the other men.

Elora settled herself on a tree stump, intending to be a firm but distant presence.

"The lake does not entice you?"

She recognized the man to be one of Gerard's men. "Excuse me, I do not believe we've been..."

"Sir Owain, m'lady." He bowed his head. "I accompanied Gerard during the king's campaigns."

Elora shifted across the log to allow room for Owain. "And what brings you back to Edan? Are the campaigns finally over?"

"Without the king to pursue them, yes. Gerard wished to return home, and we travel together, so Edan, here we are."

"You do not miss the fighting?"

"I welcome a warm bed, a sumptuous meal, and the cheery atmosphere of a cozy castle. It is favorable to sleeping in the damp rain, washing in the mud, and moving from place to place with no end in sight. 'Tis for a noble cause, but..."

"You grew disheartened."

Owain tilted his head. "Indeed."

"And Gerard...?"

"His music kept us all sane during a time of despair." He rubbed the back of his neck. "Truth be told, homesickness took hold. Thus, he expressed the desire to settle down."

She blinked. Did Gerard wish to marry? Have children? Had he already a beau? Her heart ached once more and wished for the privacy of her bedchamber. Still, she contented herself to enjoy the warmth of the late summer evening. She looked up at the sky, where both moon and sun co-existed. It would not be long before daylight left them.

Commotion from the men drew her eyes to the water. She grimaced as each man took turns to strike a shield with their lance, whilst standing on a boat.

"Do your men not think this a dangerous venture on the eve before their tournament?"

"Danger? Mere sport, 'tis all."

She swallowed her concerns and nodded, forcing a smile to tell herself all would be well. "But they have drunk much this eventide. Surely 'twould be more sensible for them to get abed early?"

Owain laughed and studied her features. "I can see why he was so taken with you."

His response caught in her throat. Did he speak of Gerard? She noted his use of past tense.

"Does Sir Gerard have a... did he ever...?"

The resounding crack of a lance ripped into the vessel's shield. One boat crashed into another as wood scraping upon wood vibrated across the water. The body of a man thudded onto the deck. Aimee cried out in alarm.

Instinctively, Elora gathered her skirts and ran toward the

tragedy.

Shouting surrounded Gerard as they pulled him from the boat. Had he done this? Gerard couldn't remember. Everything blurred as the noise enveloped him. Gerard blinked at Elora's concerned face hovering above him, her flaxen hair shining in the moonlight. She briefly cupped his face and touched his forehead. Then she nodded to someone else. Owain?

Yes, his friend's deep voice resounded in the depths of Gerard's skull. They hurled him onto a horse and rushed him to the castle. Every part of him ached. Night ascended fast. The whoosh of a burning torch light struck out as they passed through the massive doors.

They entered the infirmary, but he did not see Gias, Carisleau's physician, anywhere. Mayhap the man was abed, like any other normal person at this hour. He stared down at his crumpled hand and looked away immediately. Not good at all.

"How will I play for the queen's feast?"

"Hush, now." Elora poured strong wine down his throat. "Gerard, you've injured your hand. This might hurt a little."

Pain shot up his arm as she prodded and examined him. More men brought in Ambrose and laid him on a pallet nearby with Gias close behind.

Elora spoke in a hushed tone as the physician neared. "I will give him some willow bark to ease his discomfort."

Slumber came readily, but not for long. The pain would not stay at bay. As people came and went throughout the night, Gerard tossed and turned in his sleep. But Elora stayed through, grinding down treatments, and checking on him periodically.

She sat beside him, her gentle touch a reminder of her quiet and caring nature. His heart began to ache. All this time—had he never stopped loving her?

A man entered the chamber, and Elora walked over to him, speaking in soft whispers. She seemed unusually familiar with him, and he with her. Gerard leaned closer, straining his ears to hear their mumblings.

"I heard there'd been an incident, my lady, and I knew you'd be the first here and the last to leave."

"I am fine, Mathias. There is no need to trouble yourself over me. I shall get some rest in the morning. Gias will need his sleep tonight, for he'll be required tomorrow as the tournament begins."

"Why must anyone stay? These are superficial injuries."

"Mayhap, but their pain does not leave. I am here to do something about it."

"Your astute care does you credit, my lady. You are the most selfless person I know."

Elora waved him off with her hand. "Nonsense, I keep busy for myself. I cannot stand to be idle. Now, there is no need for the both of us losing sleep this night. Do you not have duties in the garrison?"

"No, all is quiet, but I shall leave if you're sure all is well."

"Good night, Mathias."

As Elora's footsteps neared, Gerard closed his eyes. He had so many questions he wished to ask her, but the throbbing in his head prevented him from thinking clearly, let alone stringing together a coherent conversation. Even so, the years apart had deepened the gap between them, and now they acted like strangers. He dare not assume there were no other beaus in Elora's life.

Such unsettling notions, more so than the pain, gave cause for a troubled sleep.

~

"Have you been here all night?"

At the sound of Aimee's voice, Elora stretched out her arms and eased the tired ache from her neck. "I could not leave him."

Aimee snorted. "You're not in a convent any longer, Cousin. We have servants for things like this. Where is Gias?"

"I sent him to his chamber for rest."

"And you? When will you sleep?"

"I am touched by your concern, but I assure you, I have endured many a sleepless night before, and I doubt this shall be my last."

"Then I need you to accompany me to the joust this day."

Elora inwardly groaned. "You know how violence displeases me so. I take no pleasure in watching good men injure themselves for entertainment." She glanced at the troubadour lying still on his pallet.

"But you have to be there. I cannot sit in the box all by myself. People will think I have no friends."

Elora quirked her brow. "Dear one, we have a castle full of people, and you've many ladies at your disposal. Take Lydia with you."

"But Lydia is so... demanding."

Elora stifled a grunt. The irony that Aimee's dearest friend could be difficult when Aimee was, at times, one of the most trying maidens in the kingdom, touched her as a little amusing.

"If you do not accompany Lydia, whom will she sit next to?"

Aimee rolled her eyes. "Very well, I shall offer to go with her, but only because I'm a good Christian woman. Although, I see it conveniently frees you to be absent. Father will not be so pleased. How will you find an eligible suitor if you do not acquaint yourself in society?"

"I am not looking for a suitor, remember? Besides, Uncle won't notice my absence if you do not tell him."

"He may be blind, but he is not stupid."

"I know it."

Elora finished grinding the bark into powder and wiped her

hands. She missed times like these, to be put to use in a quiet place of the castle. She humored her uncle by making the odd public appearance. After all, he did truly wish to find her a suitable match, even if Aimee was the priority at the moment.

Aimee peered around the curtain at the sleeping men. "Of course, you'd rather stay in a room with handsome, helpless men at your disposal—"

"Hush now, do not be ridiculous. You forget I nearly took the vow and would have been caring for many more injured and helpless folk."

Aimee folded her arms and shook her head. "How could anyone pledge not to marry? The notion is foreign to me."

"'Tis a high calling, I warrant. Even the apostle Paul said it was better to remain unmarried but acknowledged such a choice was not the easiest of paths."

"And do you regret not staying in the nunnery?"

Elora glanced toward the curtain separating her from the men's view, fully aware that the thin material did little to prevent any sound filtering through. She lowered her voice. "I confess that I am still undecided on the matter."

Aimee gasped. "Gracious, Cousin. How can you deliberate so?"

"I returned to Carisleau to have time to ponder and... I'm still doing so."

"Well, you clearly have no interest in marriage for you've turned away every suitor that crosses your path. Mayhap you should return to the convent. Is it the teaching that you miss? Surely you can reside there and still get involved without having to promise celibacy."

"I fear it does not work like that. Granted, Aunt sent me to the Sisters of Mercy as a child primarily for my education, but it was my decision to stay on as a novice. Still, there is only so much time Madame Evangeline gives before one must decide."

"But you risk becoming an old maid. If you do not do something soon, you'll have accomplished naught."

The thought of wasting her life plagued her every day. "If the Lord has a man for me, I look forward to it. In the meantime, I will work diligently." She narrowed her eyes at her cousin. "What I accomplish for His namesake is not dependent on whether I choose to marry."

Aimee scowled. "Fair enough, and you can continue to contemplate such matters now. Only I must leave you. Please get some rest though, for it will not do for you to go to the dance this eventide with those dark circles under your eyes!"

At Elora's departure, Gerard exhaled. Had he been holding his breath all this time?

Ambrose groaned from his pallet in the corner. "Curse you, Gerard. I think I nearly died last night."

"Nonsense. You were the one who rammed your boat into the shield. It was my hand that was damaged." He glanced down at his bandaged fingers. Would he ever play again? "Other than banging your head and swallowing a fair amount of water, you remain remarkably unscathed."

Ambrose patted down his body. "You mean I am uninjured?"

"Seem to be."

"God be praised—I can assist Owain in the joust this day."

"Not so fast, good men." Gias peered around the corner. "Your head took a collision. I'd prefer you to stay and rest—"

"Your preference and my purse might disagree. I'll not win my share of any prize money sat in the infirmary." Ambrose hurried to dress.

The physician cocked an eyebrow. "Then you'd best hasten, for I can hear the herald already."

Ambrose darted out of the chamber.

"How is it his clumsiness has cost me, not him?" Gerard groaned.

Gias took Gerard's hand and carefully unwound the bandage. "Do you remember what happened?"

Gerard thought back to the previous evening. "I only jumped aboard the boat because I saw how Ambrose was behaving. We'd all had far too much to drink, and spirits were high. What were they all thinking, playing water shields the night before the tournament?"

"Indeed, your valor comes at a price."

Gerard swallowed. "Is it broken?"

"No, but you'll not be able to move your fingers until the swelling comes down."

"How long until my hand heals?"

Gias shook his head. "Hard to say, but you cannot play your instruments this week."

Gerard drew a sharp intake of breath. "Unable to perform, or simply shouldn't?"

"What is the difference?"

"A great deal. If I can play through the pain, it is worth it. But if I'll damage my hand in doing so..."

"You'll need to enlist some help. You still have your voice, at least."

"But the people do not flock here from across the kingdom to hear just anyone play my songs." He pressed his good hand against his chest. "They expect to see me."

"And they will, but just singing. Leave the instruments to the others."

"And how will I explain this to the queen? I've received a large commission to put on the greatest musical performance of the year in memory of the king."

Gias wrinkled his brow. "I suggest you get praying for a miracle."

A miracle indeed.

Chapter Three

Rays of sun beamed down upon the jousting arena on the first day of the tournament. A gentle summer breeze swept across Elora's face, loosening a tendril of hair. She tucked it back up into her gold net and glanced across the tournament box. After having rested the morning away, she felt obligated to at attend the remainder of the day's activities. Her stomach fluttered at Gerard's approach.

"My lady," greeted Gerard as he entered the tournament box. Elora forced a smile and tapped her uncle's arm. "Uncle, Sir Gerard is here."

"My lord."

"Ah, Gerard. I heard you've encountered some trouble. It won't bear any consequence to your music, I trust."

"That is the reason for my visit..."

Gerard sat on the bench next to Elora, and her mouth turned dry. Unlike the other knights surrounding them, who dressed in full ceremonial armor, he wore a smart tunic and hose, which only accentuated his muscular physique.

Sweat formed on her brow, and she edged further away from

him, thankful she remained seated. No doubt her legs would have buckled beneath her had she been standing.

"I crushed my hand last night between the boat and the water shield. Your physician has seen to me, and has it well bandaged, but I cannot play my lute or vielle."

"But the queen—"

"I can still sing, my lord, and we can use minstrels to accompany me. I'll teach them my songs. Your castle performers do read music, yes?"

Lord Reginald spat. "Common folk have no need for it. But Elora does..."

Elora's heart pounded. "Only for the portative organ, Uncle."

"You also play the harp, no?" Gerard turned to look at her, his piercing gaze matched her own.

She gave an awkward nod. "I did a long time ago, but I am much out of practice."

"Then you will help me?"

The earnest tone of his voice cut through to her heart. Yes, they had an unresolved past, but like it or not, they would face it from this moment. The queen's wishes took precedent.

Aunt Beatrice cleared her throat and placed a hand on Uncle Reginald's knee. "My dear, you know how Elora detests performing. It goes against her upbringing. Is that not so? It would not be fair to draw so much attention on our niece when she does not wish it. There are other far more accomplished musicians who can assist Gerard, should he need more."

Elora's heart thumped faster. It was nice for her aunt to look out for her, but she had a voice, and indeed the choice was her own to make. It stung that Aunt Beatrice didn't think her own accomplishments rivaled Gerard's.

She looked across at his concerned face, taking the moment to savor in his gaze. "I am happy to assist you in hiring local minstrels. Indeed, I know of some who can pick up melodies quickly and learn by ear whatever it is you wish them to play. Let us go now, if it suits you."

Without waiting for a response, Elora rose to leave, not daring to look back to see if he accompanied her. She needed to get out of this box before it stifled her.

Gerard picked up his pace, following Elora out of the tournament stands. "Where are we going?"

"The village tavern. There are some minstrels there I would like to introduce you to. We often use them at our functions and they're extremely good."

Gerard reached out and placed a hand on her arm, causing her to falter. "Do not listen to your aunt. You are one of the most musical people I know."

"She did not mean anything by it. She merely wished to rescue me from performing against my will."

Gerard scoffed. He doubted that. More likely, Lady Beatrice didn't want the attention to move away from Aimee and land on Elora. She'd always had a way to bestow a compliment with an underlying criticism. Still, he knew Elora tried to see the best in people, and she would not hear of anything negative about her aunt, so he held his tongue.

They entered the half-empty establishment and followed the sound of stringed instruments through to the back room. A man sat in the corner playing on his gittern. His technique could be better, and he lacked a degree of presence, but he certainly had a sense of musicality.

"Wilhelm, this is..."

At the sight of Gerard, Wilhelm almost dropped his instrument. He staggered up and shook Gerard's good hand in a brash manner.

"The great Gerard de Castille, what an absolute honor."

"Please, carry on."

Wilhelm's face turned red as he nodded. Returning to his fellows, they continued their ensemble and Gerard listened with interest. He himself had been taught by the prestigious composers of the kingdom—a breed of elite men that studied the complexities of composition and sought to instill meaning within each piece. At such a level, inevitably, their music became almost sacred, so far out of reach of the people that it risked becoming irrelevant. But the music of the common folk sounded faster, lighter, and carried the tales of old, passed down from generation to generation.

He glanced toward Elora. They had enjoyed many outdoor country dances during the summer of their youth, but both had much changed. He longed to talk with her, to ask her outright why after her initial rejection she'd not pursued the very dream which forced them apart. For now, he would have to content himself with merely being with her. As they sat and listened, Elora drummed her fingers to the rhythm.

"Why did you stop playing the harp?"

She glanced up, her amber eyes fluttering wide open. "I had no teacher."

"I can teach you now."

Her bright eyes widened. "In a week? Do you not move on after the tournament?"

He didn't want to, no. But he went wherever commissioned. "My plans are as yet undecided."

He would not mention that his fellow knights were planning on touring the knight's circuit. It was true. He'd not yet decided whether to go with them.

"Where is everyone?" He motioned toward the empty tavern.

"They're all watching the joust, and although still considered a preliminary event, folk around here enjoy it more than the rest of the competition. Even women spectate, as I'm sure you've noticed."

"And you? I recall you never enjoyed seeing people hurt."

"A sentiment we both shared, I once thought."

Gerard shrugged. "To unnecessary killing, yes. But men need to train and fighting for sport enables this. I confess, I prefer a tournament to the raw danger of a battlefield, even though the joust is a mere mockery of the actuality of war. All the color, pomp, and ceremony, the knights' code of conduct... it all goes to the wind when you're in the center an actual battle."

Elora gasped. "Did you fight with your comrades? I'd presumed you were there as a musician—"

"I had to. See, I bear the marks." He pointed to the scar upon his chin and the ones on his palm. "There are more, but..." Shaking the unpleasant memories of his time on the king's campaign, he tapped the table and rose. "I've heard enough. These men I can work with, if they are willing. We'll rehearse after nones. Are you able to join us?"

She drew in a breath. "Yes, I'll make time to be there."

"No, no, no... this is all wrong." Gerard waved his hands mid-air in frustration.

Elora paused, longing to intervene but not thinking it her place to do so. The minstrels she'd help gather sat on the performance balcony with their instruments raised. But they did not grasp Gerard's particular rhythm, nor remember the melody. Gerard used his voice to hum the tune, and she would demonstrate again on her organ, but Gerard's unique music deemed far too complicated for them. They'd been rehearsing all afternoon, and they were due to perform this very evening.

"They'll not be ready in time. You will have to play for me this evening, Elora."

Elora nearly gawped. "Me? Only me?"

"I'll be here, of course, singing, but this ensemble requires much work before the queen's feast."

She placed a hand upon her beating heart, as if the pressure would calm her concerns. "I do not perform."

Gerard spun and faced her, studying her countenance. It was the first time they'd really locked eyes since his arrival. She pictured a younger Gerard, before he'd been to war, when they'd talked of their hopes and dreams for the future. Memories of their times spent by the springs, making music together, returned. She'd not been shy then. Not in front of him.

He tilted his head in a questioning fashion.

"I play for God, not..." She glanced around, frustrated at her own feeble words, unable to voice her uncomfortableness without laying offense at his own profession. The church often scorned at what society classed as 'entertainment' and even desired to ban dancing. She did not hold the same views, however, she did not wish to be disloyal to her upbringing.

"Do it for Him then, not I, but please, do not abandon me now, Lorie."

At his change in tone, and his soft approach as he spoke her childhood name, she hesitated. Aware of the other eyes upon her, she merely nodded.

Gerard dismissed the musicians with the clap of his hands.

"So, for tonight I'd like to perform this song." He motioned toward the sheet music.

Elora picked up the faded parchment with trepidation. The notes she recognized, but... "What are these markings here?"

"That is the rhythm. These denote the mode, and these the melody, but the darker the note, the shorter it holds for."

She sucked in her breath. "This is new... we do not write the music like this at Sisters of Mercy."

"No indeed. 'Tis complicated but more accurate in annotation and means our songs will exist for years. Here, let me show you." Gerard sat next to her, his arm brushing against her own. He pointed to the notes as he sang, "da de da de da de dum..." tapping his other hand upon his thigh. "You see?"

She nodded, then played the organ along with his singing. This additional way of reading music would take some practice. Still, she'd no longer need to remember by rote the rhythmic patterns of the piece. It would certainly enable musicians to create more complex compositions.

"You learned much from Master Francis?"

His eyes lit up. "I did, and so much more than we talked about. I only wish you could have been there..." He stopped himself before finishing the sentence off, which she could only assume would be, *but you chose the convent over me.*

She wasn't ready to give her reasons to him and so instead turned her attention to the music, jutting out her tongue in concentration. "This melody is beautiful. Where did you draw your inspiration?"

Gerard hesitated. "Anywhere and everywhere. The rustle of the leaves on the trees, the trickling of the stream, nearby laughter... it's God's own music, is it not?"

She smiled at his enthusiasm. "I too am inspired by creation. Making music inside a drafty hall is probably not the best place to—"

"Then let's leave." He took the organ and placed it carefully on the dais. "Come."

Unable to resist his eager face, Elora followed him through the corridor, past the tournament crowds, and along the embankment down to the river. She laughed as they sped downward. The wind freed her hair and excitement warmed her cheeks. They stopped by the stream, and Elora cupped her hands to sip the ice-cold water, despite the warmth of the day.

"Never ceases to amaze me how cool this spring water stays."

"Or how sweet it is," replied Gerard. "There is no water across the three Caragh kingdoms that tastes quite like it."

"Truly?" She sat straighter and studied him. He'd flicked his legs up, crossed lazily over a rock, his back on the ground, and arms resting behind his head. It was as if no years had passed between them, that they were as before, enjoying the summer at Carisleau.

"You traveled far on the campaigns?"

"Yes."

"What do you think happened to the king? Some say he was never captured... that he roams the kingdom in deliberate exile, choosing a free life over duty."

Gerard shrugged. "War is so extreme, 'tis enough to break any man, rich or poor. Did King Robert? I do not know, but his duty to the people drove his every breath. Alas, such a heavy weight can be burdensome."

Elora knelt beside him. "You talk as if you knew him personally. Were you not just one of many knights under his campaign?"

"No, I was one of his three personal guards. My role was to accompany him on his missions, so I had the ultimate responsibility of ensuring his safety."

Elora picked a daisy from the grass, made a hole in the stalk, and threaded another flower through. "And how does an esteemed troubadour become the king's protector?"

Gerard arched one eyebrow as a lopsided grin formed. "I was playing for the king in Morgandy when we came under attack." He shrugged. "I saved his life, and he requested I join the royal guard."

"But you've never been one for violence—"

"Lorie, you know as well as I, you do not say no to the king. Besides, I continued as a troubadour on our campaigns. The king loved my music."

"Then what happened? How did the king disappear?"

"In a battle. We did not find his body, nor did any ransom request come forward. And we searched for months. In the beginning, I determined not to return without him, but as the days progressed, the soldiers grew discouraged, and we had to face reality."

She exhaled. "How tragic."

Gerard glanced at the soft white clouds overhead. "I find my only solace in music."

"Where have you been?"

Elora stared in the looking glass to see Aimee's reflection. She returned her attention to Clarice as she wove gold threads through her hair and positioned them up around her ears. "No, Clarice. Pin them to the back. I cannot hear a thing if my hair covers my ears." She glanced back at Aimee. "I was with Sir Gerard."

"By yourself?" The shock in her tone did not go amiss. "And all day?"

"I was not alone, for the most part. I've been helping him with his music since he cannot play himself."

Aimee folded her arms. "I presume it was Gerard and your army of invisible soldiers that I saw gallivanting off in the countryside this afternoon."

"Were you spying on me, Cousin?"

Aimee tapped her foot.

"Yes, we went to the brook for a while, but naught improper occurred, I can assure you. We are old friends, you understand."

"You are? How did you ever meet? He left Carisleau Castle before you returned from the convent."

"Do you not remember that summer when you and Uncle visited Morgandy? I returned to Carisleau after finishing my education to care for Aunt in your absence. Aunt kept mostly to her chamber, and I really had naught to do."

"Cousin, what are you trying to tell me? You met Gerard and…?"

Elora sighed. "And naught, I suppose. He saw me practicing the harp and offered to tutor me. I spent the summer here, then I returned to the nunnery to become a novice nun and he went off to learn under Master Francis."

Aimee sat on the bed and blinked. "He is the reason you could never take the vow. You fell in love with him, didn't you?"

"Oh nonsense. I was just a child. Too young to comprehend my own heart."

"But do you know it now?"

Elora placed a hand on her pounding chest. "Does a lady ever truly know? Now, you must ready yourself for this evening. Be off with you. I'll send Clarice through to you in a moment."

Aimee folded her arms, as if waiting for more information. But Elora would not give it. She could scarcely think it herself.

Her cousin exited in a huff.

Elora glanced at Clarice and her quivering hands. "You are quiet this eventide. Is all well with your family?"

Clarice's eyes darted up.

"My dear, you look like a frightened fawn. Is anything untoward? Were the leftovers I sent to them not enough?"

"My family is ever grateful. It's just…"

Elora patted the space beside her on the bench and motioned for Clarice to sit down. "You do not wish to betray your family's confidence, I understand. Nor do you want to compromise your position here. But I hope you feel able to confide in me if you need help."

"Tha-thank you, my lady."

Elora stared at her maid. There was something going on that the girl dared not share. She'd mention it to her uncle. Mayhap more could be done for their people.

Once ready, Elora slipped into the hall to watch the dancing from the sidelines. She found a pleasant corner with a good vantage point. Here she settled down to enjoy the music, tapping her foot along with the beat. She scoured the line-up of dancers. A nice balance of men and women enabled an array of different dances to take place. Growing up in the convent, she was not adept at many of them, and her lack of confidence often prevented her from joining in.

"Come, Lorie, I would have you dance."

Her cousin's overly loud voice startled her. She sent a warning stare, but Aimee played ignorant until she had reeled off a list of good men willing to dance with her. "Mathias, I am sure would be eager to—"

Relief flooded as Gerard suddenly appeared at her side and took her hand.

"Thank you, I thought for a moment I would have to—" She hesitated as Gerard escorted her into the center of the room. "Gerard, you know I cannot dance. I assumed you were rescuing me from an embarrassing situation."

Gerard leaned down and whispered in her ear. "I am saving you from yourself, for, as memory serves, you can indeed dance." He signaled the minstrels to play, and Elora could do naught but oblige him.

Her heart pulsated as the music changed from the faster reel to the slower paced Swan Dance. Now this one she knew. It was the last dance that she and Gerald had enjoyed before they'd departed. At the thought, an unwelcome tear escaped down her cheek. A breath caught in her throat as their hands met momentarily, and then they were pulled away. How her legs remembered the steps was beyond her.

"See, you dance well."

Their paths crossed diagonally, and their fingers touched briefly once more. She twirled away, crisscrossing along the line, and again into the center. Back towards him. He pulled her closer, closer than he should have, until their faces almost touched. Dark silken hair framed his face, and she found herself drawn into his hazel eyes.

The music ended abruptly, and she waited eagerly to see if Gerard would instigate another dance with her.

"My lady," cut in Mathias's voice, slicing through the moment like he'd just poured an ice-cold pail of water over them. "May I have this next dance?"

Gerard, cloaked in dignity, simply bowed and stepped back, allowing Mathias to take Elora's hand. How willingly Gerard let her go hurt deeply. Why had she ever let him go?

Chapter Four

The third day of the tournament began at full pace, with the final rounds of jousting, sword one-on-one combat, and freestyle events. Then there would be two days of rest before the melee finale on day six. Elora blew a wisp of hair from her face as she wrapped another bandage around Owain's upper arm. He grimaced as she secured it.

"Why do you do it?"

Owain frowned. "Truly, you need ask? The knight's ideal is the mere essence of manhood. We fight to prove our worth."

She laughed. "And I suppose the bag of coins at the end of it softens the blow."

"Indeed, and the extra female attention does not go unwanted."

"But does uncertain death not deter you at all?"

"Our lances are tipped. There is no real danger."

Elora crossed her arms. "I think your damaged shoulder would argue with that."

"Naught a bandage and a bit of ointment can't cure. I can still compete in the melee by week's end, yes?"

"You'll be alive, if that is what you're asking, but possibly at a significant risk. Can you fight with an injured shoulder?"

"Of course," he scorned. "As long as my limbs are intact. I wear my armor—that's all a soldier can ask for. You'll join us too, Gerard? We could use your help on the team."

At the mention of Gerard's name, Elora's cheeks turned warm. How long had he been standing there?

His footfall across the floor drew closer. "Lord Reginald already has plenty of knights in his retinue. He does not need another. Besides, if my hand is too injured to play the lute, I think we can safely rule out combat." He let off a quick laugh.

"Shame, you were always the best at battle strategy."

"Gracious," Elora interjected. "You make the game sound like a war."

"In many respects, it is." Gerard hovered over her. "But done in the name of honor for the lord you fight for."

"How can such a competition be fair?" She tried to concentrate on Owain's shoulder and calm her heartbeat.

"Oh, there are marshals." Owain shifted his weight on the bench. "But they cannot be around for it all. Its danger is a reason the event has ceased in many other kingdoms."

"Then why does my uncle permit the melee at Carisleau?"

"To honor the king's memory. Even though he is not here, the queen wishes it to continue. King Robert always loved an exciting melee."

Elora packed away her supplies and washed her hands. "Phew, I think that sees to everyone until the next event." She squeezed Gias's arm as she left the infirmary tent and breathed in the fresh air. Owain and Gerard followed her out.

Elora glanced at the sun's shadows. "Gracious, what time is it? I only stopped by briefly to help Gias, but I see the day has passed."

"'Tis the middle of the morning."

Elora cast her gaze along the makeshift marketplace outside

the castle grounds. Stalls of myriad color punctuated the land-scape as on market day, only instead of the usual goods on display, blacksmiths, outdoor taverns, and armory took their place. They walked along one row and passed by acrobats, dancers, and then country minstrels. Crowds of varied class filtered through from the spectator stands and intermingled. Someone playing the pipe caught Gerard's eye, so he stopped to listen with measured intent. Owain grew bored and found a group of ladies in which to share his knightly escapades. Elora just stood in the center of it all, absorbing the cacophony of sounds. She interpreted them into a rhythm and melody the way she used to do as a child.

Gerard turned to her without a word. They continued walking along the street. "That tune... what is it?"

Elora blinked, unaware she'd been humming, and shrugged. "A simple melody that entered my head."

"We need to write this down." With urgency, he pushed past a cleric taking inventory on the side and snatched his wax tablet.

"Da da di da di da..." he echoed after her and started scrib-bling. "It's brilliant. A melodic genius, in fact."

Elora mouthed a brief apology to the castle steward and slipped him coinage for his tablet. They walked on.

"Now for some words... any kind of divine inspiration?"

"The lines from my prayer book would fit nicely... *The Lord is my comfort and keeper, His strength, a pillar, hallelujah...*"

Gerard quirked his upper lip. "That could work." And as Elora sang, Gerard started singing in a lower register, "da da di di da da..."

Elora paused. "Your harmony is most unusual."

His eyes sparkled. "That's what makes it so wonderful, do you not think? Now I'm going to sing different words over yours. Let's try a love poem... *White petals wilt not, her elegance exudes...*"

As Elora continued to sing her melody to the words of her

prayer, Gerard sung his poem, with longer drawn-out notes, on top of her own. The contrast, yet unexpected synergy, formed a magnificent musical tapestry, and she stopped singing just to hear his love song. Who was the white rose? Had Gerard ever loved another after her? The thought became almost too painful to bear.

Her stomach rumbled just as the midday bell rang, calling them to eat. Gerard took her arm in his. They headed for the field between the castle and the forest. Elora ran her hands through the flowers as they walked. Blue, violet, and yellow hues dotted the otherwise green landscape. She inhaled the summer scent while savoring the quiet moment.

"Here." Gerard plucked a wildflower and tucked it in her hair.

She touched it and felt her face heat.

Over twenty banqueting tents proudly stood for the knights and ladies to dine. Elora eyed the line of guards and pursed her lips. Seeing Mathias, she moved over to him.

"Is it necessary to guard a field?"

Mathias's mouth twitched and then formed a smile. "Your uncle's orders, my lady. He is fearful that, with so many common folk close by, they might try to steal all the food."

A little surprised at Lord Reginald's instructions, she moved toward the largest of all the tents, and pulled back the fabric. She exhaled at the sight of the banquet. Rows of tables covered in crisp white linen and adorned with forest greenery consumed the area. Her eyes widened further as her gaze extended to the plentiful amount of food gracing the platters. A banquet indeed.

She recalled Jesus's teaching on a wedding banquet where the host had invited all near and far to participate.

"'Tis a shame the feast could not be extended to all the spectators this day. There is surely enough food to be had for all. The leftovers would only be passed on to them in the end." She made a mental note to talk privately with her aunt and uncle about the matter. But there was naught that could be done now. Sighing, they headed for the dais and joined Lord Reginald, Lady Beatrice, and Aimee.

"Ah, there you are, my dear. I'm glad you've joined us."

"How did you recognize me, Uncle?"

Uncle Reginald tapped her hand. "You have a certain scent about you."

Elora gasped. "You infer I smell?"

The smile lines lit up around Reginald's eyes, but he made no comeback response. He'd riled her, which was always his intent.

"Lily of the Valley," Gerald whispered near her ear and at her questioning eyebrow he then replied, "I've known no other to wear it."

She could only hope his response to be a compliment. Heat rising once more to her face, she turned to her seat, then her smile faded at her aunt's cold stare.

"Nice of you to make an appearance, dear," Lady Beatrice declared with a forced smile. "If a little late."

"Forgive me, Aunt. I lost all sense of time." Elora's cheeks blushed as she glanced to the floor.

Gerard witnessed Elora immediately retreat within herself. A cursory glance at Lady Beatrice confirmed his suspicions. The control that woman seemed to have over her niece was staggering. He suspected her aunt had put a stop to any potential nuptials between them all those years ago. Although he could not, for the life of him, fathom why. Was he so disagreeable? So below their social status?

"As you can see, we have already started. You missed the blessing." Beatrice motioned a page boy over with a platter of food.

Elora took care to place her napkin over her arm and retrieve the knife from her girdle. "Thank you, Godwin."

Not waiting to be served, Gerard waved the page off. "Worry not, lad. I'll fetch my own."

When it came to food, he knew what he liked, and indeed did not. He headed for the banqueting table, grabbed an extra-large platter, and proceeded to load his plate with various succulent meats, pies, and bread.

Upon his return, Elora's eyes had reddened. He glanced across to Beatrice, who had now angled herself toward the other end of the table.

"Here," he said tenderly, and deposited a slice of pork pie onto her plate.

She smiled, and her shoulders relaxed. She cut a look across the table, and then quickly scooped several slices of venison onto his own platter. She remembered his favorite meat. The small act warmed his heart.

Then Elora tapped a rhythm with her fingers on the table, so quiet only he could hear it above the surrounding noise. He grinned. She continued their song from earlier. The song which had made them both late for the midday meal. He joined in, with his hand resting just beside hers, tapping out his corresponding part.

The corner of her mouth turned up.

"And what will you perform this eventide, Sir Gerard?" Lord Reginald's voice broke their rhythm.

Elora paused in her tapping and feigned interest in the grooves of her knife.

Gerard leaned toward his host. "I am open to suggestions, my lord."

"Then it depends on the state of your hand. Is it healed enough to play?"

Gerard flexed his fingers. He could move them, but they still hurt. "I will not risk it yet, but Elora has indeed been a godsend. There is none of my repertoire that cannot be performed."

"Then I look forward to whatever you choose for us."

Lady Beatrice cleared her throat. "Our minstrels are adequate, so you surely do not need Elora's assistance, Sir Gerard. She does so prefer to remain in the background."

"Lady Elora is one of the best musicians I have ever had pleasure to play with. Alas, I heed your words, and shall leave Elora's participation entirely up to her." He turned to Elora and studied her countenance. Her own music synchronized with his so perfectly—he had never played with anyone else who met her match so equally.

Her eyes fluttered up to his, and she held his gaze. "My aunt is right. I do not usually perform. But how can I pass up this opportunity to play with the great Sir Gerard de Castille, commissioned by my queen? I would be honored to take part, if it pleases you."

Gerard swallowed. "Then we will rehearse after the jousting finale. I look forward to it."

The crowds cheered and waved. Small children dangled off the wooden fences, desperate to get a closer view of their hopeful champion. The drums beat louder and faster, and the spectators joined with stamping their feet.

Elora scanned the rows of peasants at the back, then along the lines of soldiers, knights, and other ranks of nobility. The bright colors made the whole event look like a painting. It seemed the entire kingdom had crammed into the small confines of Carisleau grounds.

The two knights waited, one at each end, with their lances poised. Their horses grew restless, but they had to wait for the flag to fall. The knight in the dark blue had Aimee's handkerchief tied onto the back of his helmet.

"Is that Owain?" Elora asked Gerard, and he nodded.

"But he is injured. Surely, he cannot—"

Gerard's jaw clenched. "They're all hurt but are aware of the risks."

"And who is his opponent?"

"He's only known as The Gray Knight. He will not reveal his name."

Aimee leaned across. "How mysterious. I wonder if he is handsome."

"I am surprised, dear cousin, that you gave your token to Sir Owain and not this Gray Knight instead."

Aimee snorted. "I would have done, had he accepted it."

Elora glanced at Gerard with a knowing smile. "Mayhap it is best then that you save yourself any angst about it and console his rejection by imagining his appearance to be lacking."

The flag lowered, and both knights charged forward, their lances raised. Owain's shoulder sagged, and his lance along with it.

"Come on..." muttered Gerard. "Come on..."

Elora squinted as the knights' weapons collided, and their heads flung back to avoid any fatal blow. She exhaled as they passed by each other and returned to the other side, ready to take another go.

"At least Owain was not de-horsed."

"But neither was The Gray. Still, Owain will get points for striking his chest."

As the crowds settled, Elora turned to Lord Reginald. "Uncle, about the banqueting tents and quantities of food..."

She paused as Reginald angled his ear towards the jousting.

"What's happening?" Impatience etched his voice.

"The flag has lowered." Elora held her breath as Owain set-off a fraction faster than The Gray.

"His hold is good..." Gerard raised his head.

Elora nodded, clenching her fists tighter.

Gerard tensed. "Something's wrong."

Owain flung from his horse. But even before she could cry out or run to his side to help, the wooden spectator stands shook, and the ground rumbled. She froze in unbelief at the sight before her.

Were they under attack?

Chapter Five

Arrows soared from above, and the tournament area swarmed with fighting peasants with axes and pitchforks. It took Elora a few moments for the realization to surface. They were under attack by their own people.

"We must get you to safety," shouted Gerard. "Follow me."

Shaking off the overwhelming desire to hide, Elora took her uncle's hand and shooed her cousin down the stairs. But as they reached the bottom and started for the gatehouse, Elora glanced back.

"No," shouted Aimee, "the castle is the safest place—"

"We cannot leave Owain!"

Gerard glanced at Lord Reginald and Lady Aimee, and back to the jousting ground, torn between helping his friend and his duty in protecting the lord of the land.

But Elora seized his hesitation and ran toward the fighting.

Heaven above help them. He motioned for Reginald and Aimee to hide under a bench and then ran after Elora. Not dressed for warfare, he did not even carry a sword. As he pursued Elora, he grabbed the end of a broken lance, and paved the way for Elora's safety. He'd thought his fighting days were behind him, but once a knight, always a knight.

A peasant hurtled their weight toward him. He ducked and stabbed with his lance, continuing forward. There was little time to think. His senses dulled as his only focus became retrieving Owain and keeping Elora safe.

"Help me lift him."

A cursory glance surveyed Owain's wounds. He still had part of the lance jutting out of his side. With care, Gerard slung his friend over his shoulder, and using Owain's own sword, fought his way out of the grounds.

"Keep close."

Elora remained behind him, clasping his belt as they forced their way through.

"Where are your kin?"

He scoured the area for signs of Reginald and Aimee, frustrated that no one in their family ever seemed to stay put.

A flash of Aimee's gown caught his attention. Instead of heading for the castle, they escaped to the forest, with Aimee screaming as they went.

"We must run." He pointed his blade toward her cousin. She nodded, lifted the hem of her dress, and sprinted forward. He kept a few feet in front, slicing his way through. Carrying Owain's weight across his back did not make the task easy, along with the awareness that Elora had no fighting skills.

When they reached the tree line, Aimee beckoned them over. "We should go to the falls. We'll be safe there."

Of course. A cave lay hidden behind the rush of the falls. It had been many years since he'd visited their hideout. He glanced behind them. It would be safer to venture further into the woods than brave the plains leading to the castle. Who knew if their enemy had seized control of it?

He nodded and followed Aimee through the thicket toward

the springs, traveling slower on account of Reginald. Elora lingered behind. She looked awfully pale.

Finally, they came to a clearing, and the trickling sound of water followed. As they climbed the stones near the caves, the memories flooded back.

"Do you still have—"

Elora nodded. "Yes, it's well stocked."

As they entered the cave, Aimee headed for the covered chests and pulled out furs, making it comfortable for Reginald to sit. Gerard placed Owain down with relief.

"Will you help me strip his armor off?" Elora cast her gaze to Aimee. "Fetch water, yarrow, and anything else you can think of."

Together, they removed Owain's helmet, shoulder piece, and chest piece. Gerard ripped the edges of Owain's tunic and began shredding them into strips.

"No, that is dirty. I have clean linen somewhere here. We should try to keep his wound clean." Elora set to work, and Gerard stepped back. She swiped at her forehead and examined the wound. "This will need to be cauterized. Can you prepare a fire?"

Now that he could do. He exited in search of dry wood. As the sun warmed his face, he took just a moment to catch his breath, allowing the alarming events of the morning to play out in his mind. Where was Lady Beatrice? Was she inside the castle? He hoped that whoever attacked them had not seized Carisleau too. Either way, they might be safe here for a time, although he would have to return and investigate. But first, to Owain's injury.

Once his fire was hot enough, he put in the blade of his sword. This was going to hurt. He hoped Owain still lay unconscious.

Elora placed bark in Owain's mouth to bite on and held him

steady whilst Gerard cauterized his wound. She then grimaced and touched her thigh.

"Elora, are you well?"

She blinked as her body swayed.

Gerard glanced at her blood-stained hands and back down to her dress. "Are you wounded too?"

Clarice ran to the house, fraying her dress as she stumbled. Only the pig and the few chickens they owned roamed the empty one-roomed building. Tears dropped down her cheek. This was all her fault. She should have warned Lady Elora when she'd had the chance. Now blood had been unnecessarily spilled.

Her hands shook at the realization that her family was involved in the uprising. She didn't understand the purpose of their intervention. For simple peasants to think they could go up against the land's bravest knights? The notion was utterly absurd.

She folded her arms for comfort and walked through the village. The place bustled with panic as folk fled the tournament grounds. She spotted her mama and grabbed her, drawing her into an embrace. "Praise be, I thought—"

"Do not be at ease yet, Daughter. Your father has done a terrible thing."

Dread rose, and she waited for the privacy of their house before nodding Mama to elaborate.

"What do you mean?"

"They have captured the king."

Clarice blinked, "King Robert?"

"Yes, and they've taken him for ransom."

"Are you sure it is the king?"

Mama shrugged. "I did not see the man myself. But Clarice, your father's involvement is treason."

"Where is he? Where have they taken the king?"

"I know not. They've disappeared, and I do not wish to know. And nor do you, Daughter."

Clarice gasped for air, but her lungs would not fill. "I must tell my mistress."

"No, you will be silent. This is not your error. Return to the castle once the fighting has settled, and stay well away from us, for your own sake."

✒

Gerard caught Elora in his arms as she fainted.

"Cousin?" Aimee dropped her pail of water and other supplies, and ran over to them, putting down a fur blanket for Elora to rest on. Aimee examined her body and gasped, tearing at Elora's chemise to reveal fabric seeped in blood.

"Oh, dear Lord, please help her." Aimee bound her thigh, pulling it tight.

Gerard stood, helpless. "They hurt her? Why didn't she say anything?"

Guilt and fear riddled him from within. He'd been so focused on helping his friend, what if it was at the cost of his...? He did not allow his mind to go any further. Elora had been his love, but in another lifetime. She'd made it clear to him he was not her destiny. It had taken him a long time to accept that. But even now, he pleaded with the Lord to keep her from harm.

"Here," Aimee passed the bandages to him. "You see to Owain. I'll look after Elora."

"But what do I do?"

"Bandage him up good and tight. 'Tis all we can do, at least until Elora says otherwise. She has more knowledge of herbs than I do." She shook her head. "I can hardly believe this has happened. Elora's never adventurous enough to get into danger."

"You'll not see her climbing trees, or learning archery, no. She is shy, granted, and relishes in her solitude. But it takes the bravest of maidens to run into a battlefield when all the others are running away from it. Adventure for you is fun. For Elora, it is sacrifice."

Aimee dipped a sponge in the water to clean away the dried blood. "I think I've been able to stop the bleeding. Her wound is not deep but will need stitches." She visibly shook at the mention of the word.

"Are you up for the task, or should we cauterize it? The fire is still hot."

Aimee hesitated. "Let's ask her, shall we?" She retrieved some herbs and wafted them under Elora's nose.

"What is that?"

"I know not, but its smell is awfully repugnant. It will awaken her."

Elora stirred and winced when she moved. "My leg hurts." Her weak voice quivered as her eyes opened to see Aimee above her.

"Yes, Cousin, you seemed to have gotten yourself a battle wound. Would you like for me to stitch it?"

Elora's eyes widened. "I am adept at sewing and will leave the tiniest of scars, I'll sew it myself, thank you."

Aimee gasped. "You cannot do your own stitches! Tell her, Uncle."

"Elora is stronger than you think, Daughter. Let her try, at least."

Aimee went over to the chest and retrieved a small embroidery box. She showed it to Gerard. "We have everything out here. Elora and I have camped many a summer night over the years, have we not, Cousin."

"Yes, 'tis peaceful."

He grunted. "Well, not everything, surely. What about weaponry?"

Aimee pulled a face. "Well, mayhap not everything. A couple of knives for cooking, but that is probably about it."

"Not even a bow?"

Elora looked up, the needle in her mouth, and narrowed her eyes.

"Of course, I forget I am amongst ladies."

"Not all of us." Reginald chuckled. "But I confess to never having seen this cave before."

Aimee folded her arms. "Father, you cannot see at all."

"Ah well, there you have it."

A groan from Owain drew Gerard's attention, and he helped him sit-up. "Did I win?"

A few moments passed before he could respond. Had his friend been unaware the whole time? "No man, The Gray de-horsed you."

Owain rubbed his sullen face and grimaced. Then, as if aware of the others peering over him, he finally scoured their surroundings. "Where in the kingdom are we?"

"Do you not remember the fighting that transpired during your tournament?"

Owain's forehead wrinkled. "On that last run, a movement in the stalls distracted me. Just as I flung from my horse, the crowds turned to fighting."

Aimee reached for his hand and held it. "Thank the good Lord that we are alive. But what of Mother? We left her in her chamber. Is the castle still intact? Is it safe to return home?"

"I will go back when it is night." Gerard pressed her shoulder.

Aimee snorted. "No. You have an injured hand, remember? Elora and Owain are also hurt, and Father is blind! The only person who can truly go is me."

"You forget the dark makes no difference to me, Daughter. You may find that I have the advantage."

Gerard sighed and glanced at Elora. Her face paled again,

and her hands shook as she attended to her wound. The poor woman was clearly in shock. Only Aimee seemed to relish in all the excitement. A night's rest, though, would do them all good. "Let us eat and sleep here tonight. We can venture forth at sunrise."

Chapter Six

"WHAT ARE YOU GRINDING?" GERARD CAME OVER AS Elora mixed the herbs Aimee had gathered earlier.

"A pain relief blend for Owain." Elora added the crushed plants to the boiled water and passed to Owain.

"Easy on that concoction. I hope it will not render him unconscious when we need to return to the castle."

"I will." She spotted his hand and gasped. "Forgive me, I did not think of your wound. Here, let me look at it."

Elora motioned for him to come over, and he sat on the tree stump next to her, her closeness natural and comforting. She unraveled his bandage.

"Oh dear, the swelling has returned. I would usually tell you not to use it, but under the circumstances..."

Gerard cricked his neck both ways until it clicked. "That will not happen anytime soon. Fortunately, it is my left hand. Bad for playing, but not a problem for sword fighting. Honestly, though, it does not hurt."

For a time, they watched the embers before them, enjoying the peace at their secret retreat in the woods. Lord Reginald slept in the cave, and Aimee tended to Owain.

"I sometimes wonder..."

Gerard paused from stoking the fire and glanced up at Elora. "Go on."

"Why you fell for me, and not Aimee."

"Why would you say such a thing?"

Indeed, why would she? "I'm not fun or beautiful like her, and she would not turn down a proposal from the handsomest man in the castle."

"Just the castle? Now that hurts. You must surely extend my excellent qualities to the kingdom."

"'Tis a bit of a stretch." Elora smiled.

"Very well, the shire."

"I cannot say I know everyone in the county but, that is far more feasible."

"You are beautiful, Lorie. You are like a light that shines in the darkness, encompassing all that is good in the world, radiating it for all to see."

As Elora sat looking at him, with imploring eyes and freeness of spirit, it would be easy to seize advantage of the situation. After all, she was vulnerable and in pain, no doubt worrying about her aunt and the aftereffects of the attack earlier today.

He gazed at her lips—he had kissed them before, a long time ago. Only now they seemed fuller, and all her girlish features had matured. He sighed and pushed a golden strand of hair away from her eyes. This close to her, her face lit by the fire and the moonlight, he could even see the delicate freckles upon her nose, and the gold flecks of amber in her gaze.

"Why did you return? The last we spoke, you were convinced God had called you into a lifetime of service."

Her eyes glistened, and she hesitated. "What I told you was true. I believed becoming a nun was part of my calling, and I did become a novice. Only when it was time to take my vows, I couldn't. I couldn't promise God that I would never marry, because my heart has always belonged to you."

"But I thought you did not love me. You said you'd always imagined taking the veil."

"I was but sixteen, Gerard. I did not know my own heart. How could I? Now so many years have passed, and I fear that my uncertainty will be my downfall."

"Are you sure of your heart now?"

"Alas, my heart cannot function without my head, which confuses matters."

"I see." But he didn't, not really.

"And my head feels so strange... I should not have taken so much of Owain's herbs. I think I must rest for a moment." She leaned on him once more until he could hear her breathing deepen and turn into the tiniest of snores. He should really move her into the cave, but selfishly, he did not wish to be apart from her.

Under his breath, he hummed the familiar tune that accompanied him on his journey since leaving Carisleau, first at Morgandy, and then through the three kingdoms and across the seas to Durnin. The ebb and flow of the melody mirrored Elora's personality—quiet, calm, sometimes mysterious, other times joyful. It brought peace to his soul and a closeness to her that, until now, he thought he'd never get.

And yet, here they were. Neither of them wed, nor even betrothed. Was God giving them another chance at love? He longed to wake her up and talk some more, but instead laid her in the cavern to rest in comfort.

A twig snapping in the distance alerted his attention. Gerard stopped humming, listening out for anything untoward.

Owain rested a hand on his sword.

A faint whistle pierced the night, growing louder and louder. As the intruder neared, Gerard's skin turned cold. That tune was Elora's Song. Only his comrades would have known that melody. They'd heard him play it night after night.

"Who goes there?"

"An old friend."

The deep, familiar, resonating voice sent shivers through his body.

"We are armed. No swift movements. Step into the light, slowly."

The shadow cautiously moved forward, where a stream of light poured through the night sky.

"Lower your hood."

As the man complied, Gerard etched forward, disbelief working against his better judgment. A final step closer and he argued with himself no longer. The man's beard was longer than remembered, and his poor clothing did naught to make the fellow stand out from a crowd. But those deep evergreen eyes stood out, and the sword which hung around the man's belt caught the moonlight and confirmed what he already knew.

"Your Highness!"

Gerard and Owain dropped to the ground, their faces bowed. Aimee awoke and gasped as the man's features became apparent by the firelight.

"Sire?" Owain said. "'Tis you? Why we... we thought you to be dead."

"Please, do not bow on account of me. Sit. Your firelight drew me out of my hiding. I see you've eaten. Have you've anything left?" The man sat on the wood seat by the fire. "Not very kingly, I grant you." He looked around at their faces and nodded. "You have questions."

Questions? That was an understatement. It took all of Gerard's strength to not gawp at the man before them. They'd searched for the king for months and months. They'd lost all hope and finally gave up. The guilt which plagued Gerard daily because of his own failure... that was all for naught?

"We were captured by Durnins, as no doubt you know, but

we escaped, only to find that my army had moved on and left us stranded across the seas. We've spent all these months traveling through Caragh lands, journeying home. To pay for our travels, we joined the knight's circuit. During this week's tournament, word spread that The Gray Knight was me, and so Aidan and I switched places."

"Aidan? We thought he died too."

The king shook his head. "Only captured."

"Why did you not return to Morgandy upon your arrival in Edan? Why all this secrecy?"

King Robert accepted a bowl of stew from Aimee and took a slow sip. Then, wiping his beard with the back of his hand he continued.

"I had planned to reveal all at the queen's feast, but I've discovered much about my kingdom by remaining incognito. My anonymity has given me a great deal of power. People behave differently in the presence of a king, and so my quest to return home became much more than survival, rather my mission to discover the truth. Unfortunately, I fear this attack is the start of many..." He shook his head. "If we do not act now, we may have a revolt on our hands."

Gerard looked around. "Then where is Aidan?"

Robert hesitated. "At the onset of the uprising, he was captured. I was caught in the stampede and unable to make it safely within the castle grounds. I instead fled to the woods. Just now, I recognized your song. After all this time, my friend, we are once again reunited."

Gerard paused. "Do they think they have the King of Edan? They'll be asking for a king's ransom."

Robert nodded. "Aidan's life is as precious to me as my own."

"Then we should do all we can to retrieve Aidan. Who else is on our side? We must gather our troops and retaliate at once."

At the sound of voices coming from the campfire, Elora shook off her sleeping stupor and bolted upright. "What's going on?"

"Shh..." Aimee waved her hand, motioning Elora's silence. "You will not fathom who has appeared before us."

Viewing Aimee's stricken face, Elora knew it had to be someone of great significance. She listened to the men's conversation. They were talking about a king's ransom, gathering troops, and storming the castle.

She peeked outside the cave. Owain and Gerard conversed with someone else, but she could not ascertain his features. But by the sound of his articulate tone... Elora gasped, her hand to her mouth.

Aimee nodded vigorously. "Yes, it is the king. He is alive."

Elora blinked and rubbed her eyes. "The rumors were true? He was The Gray Knight, after all?"

"And he's been here amongst us all week. Who would have thought!"

She shook her head again. "I must have been out cold to have missed all this."

Aimee grinned. "You were, but not before you poured your heart out to Gerard and fell asleep on his shoulder."

Elora groaned at the memory. What had possessed her to be so candid?

Aimee ran fingers through her long hair. "I think our plans have changed now. Our strategy should be to regain control of Carisleau."

Elora glanced across at Reginald, and then whispered to Aimee so not to concern him. "And what about Aunt, and what has become of our people inside the castle?"

"The king has returned." Her uncle's voice answered strong and clear. "And he will have his plans. But ours must remain unchanged. Your mother is alone, and we must go to her. It is our home, and we will defend it. No matter the cost."

"What are you saying, Uncle?"

"That we return to the castle, but through the secret sally port entrance and gauge what has happened. For all we know, the castle may have been seized, and we have a duty to protect the king. Once we can be sure all is well, we'll open the gates and let him in."

Elora rose from her bedding. "Then let us make preparations to leave, for it will soon be daybreak."

"I will go with you." She turned to see Gerard in the cave entrance. He did not look pleased at their plan.

"What if you are met with opposition? Who will protect you?"

Elora moved over to him. "It is true, then? King Robert has returned?"

"I can barely believe it myself."

"Then what are your plans?"

"I will go with you to Carisleau Castle. The king will remain here until we can be sure it is safe."

"And who protects the king if met with opposition? Owain?"

"The king survived by himself all this long…"

Elora's eyes widened.

Gerard sighed. "Of course, I know that my duty is to defend him. I merely worry about your own safety."

"Endearing as it may be, your plan indicates a lack of trust that God will keep me safe."

"You wish for me to have more faith?"

"It cannot be a bad thing to desire more faith. After all, should faith not grow? Ever increasing the longer we live and serve Him?"

He gritted his teeth. "Lady Elora, you are as infuriating now as the day I met you."

She smiled and cupped his chin in a sudden moment of intimacy. "You certainly know how to bestow a lady with compliments."

His eyes warmed and his hand slipped to her waist.

As she pulled away, he caught her hand. "Very well. If there is trouble, send us a signal. We will watch the castle from the tree line."

CHAPTER SEVEN

THE CASTLE GROUNDS LOOKED DIFFERENT AT THE break of dawn, and as the sun raced with them to make it safely inside the walls, Elora's breath quickened. They passed through the catering tents that only yesterday had stood so gallantly. Now, only shredded fabric, upturned tables, and trampled food marked the same area. The pavilions also showed damage, but no deceased lay in sight. Elora did not know whether that was a good sign or not.

"How do you know where the port is, Uncle?"

"We head for the orchard, and then find the wall that is marked by an archway of flagstones."

Taking Lord Reginald's arm, she and Aimee guided him through the apple trees. Their canopies bloomed full, shielding their presence from any guard onlooking from the ramparts. Then they came to the castle's outer wall. Elora scanned the stones, looking for anything that remotely resembled an arch.

"I do not see..."

Her uncle placed both hands on the wall and traced his fingers across the grooves within the limestone. Then he paused.

"Here, the stone is coarse, do you see? The coarse stone forms an arch."

Elora blinked. How had she not noticed it before? She followed the subtle pattern, but dismay filled her. "Uncle, this pattern continues along the entire side of the wall. How do you know which one it is?"

"The sally port is the one with a double groove which points heavenward. If I'm not mistaken..." He ran his hand at the top and grinned. "This is it. Now we give it a good push. I'll need your help—disuse will make it difficult to open."

Elora and Aimee both leaned on the wall and pushed along with their uncle, but naught moved. "Uncle, are you sure this is the right place?" She wondered if Lord Reginald's memory had been affected. She had never known about such a passageway in all her time at Carisleau.

"We just need to lean further this way. When we find the right spot, it will start to give."

Elora glanced at Aimee, and she shrugged in response. Turning her attention back to the wall, Elora took a step backwards. The rising sun cast a little light upon the flagstones. Sure enough, when knowing what to look for, the coarser stones did indeed pattern arches along the bottom. Then she studied where her uncle pressed his weight. "I see, I wonder if we need to be directly parallel to the double groove..."

She pushed with all her might, and this time, the stone groaned.

"That's it, my dear niece. Let us do so again, and quickly, before anyone hears us."

They pushed again until Elora's feet nearly slipped in the grass, and a section of the stone wall turned. A click sounded, followed by a grinding noise.

The small door opened. Elora stepped inside first, then held out her hand for her uncle to pass through, then Aimee. They entered the blackened passageway.

"You lead us, Father," whispered Aimee.

They followed Reginald down the dark corridor and up the stairs.

"Why is there such an exit, Uncle? And how is it we never knew of its existence?"

"This is centuries old. The master architect during the Chaudors Dynasty, Francoise Bowyer, built the city walls of Morgandy, and some of the castles in Northern Edan. He designed the sally ports to be able to leave the castle in the event of a siege. It was also a way to attack the enemy unawares. Of course, in those days, warfare was primitive. They did not have the grand siege engines that can be used today."

"And its secrecy is to ensure the castle's fortification?"

"Indeed, my dear niece. The more people who know of such devices, the less secure the castle becomes. Thus, I must ask you both to never disclose its whereabouts to anyone else."

Their journey took them to an underground cellar where wine barrels, sacks of grain, and other foodstuffs scattered the chamber.

Aimee sighed. "Now what?"

"We are close to the infirmary." Elora recognized the odor of the medicinal herbs. "I am by far the quietest amongst us, and I'm sure I can enter the castle without drawing attention to myself. The both of you stay here until I fetch you."

Aimee jutted out her bottom lip.

"Surely you'd prefer to remain as far from danger as possible?"

"Yes, but neither do I wish to miss any of the adventure."

"This is no adventure, I assure you. Please stay. I will send word shortly."

Keeping to the shadows of the corridor, Elora headed first to the infirmary. Wounded men and women occupied pallets, tables, and floorspace. The stench of rotting flesh and human secretion became overwhelming. Didn't anyone tend to these people? She felt pulled to stay and help, but she instead journeyed onward, concerned at the lack of guards and servants. She checked the library first, which was empty as expected.

Then coughing came from the chapel. She put her head to the wood and listened. Who was in there? Taking a deep breath, she gently tried the handle. Scuffling and whispers came from inside.

"Hello? Who is in there?"

Silence.

"Father Jacob? Gias? Anyone?"

The door creaked open, and she was pulled inside. Elora stared at the wide-eyed crowd of faces as she shook the dust from her tunic.

"'Tis Lady Elora, O God be praised." Gias clasped his hands.

She frowned at the crowded room. "What are you all doing in here? Were you captured?"

"We barricaded ourselves in when the fighting started and haven't left since. Is it a blood bath out there?"

"The infirmary is full, but no one else is around. Where is my aunt?"

Gias pointed to the corner of the room.

Elora rushed to the woman. "Aunt Beatrice? Thank the Lord you are safe. We have been worried about you."

Beatrice looked up, her brow wrinkled. "Where are your uncle and cousin?"

"Waiting in the cellars. Have you supplies? Food? Water?"

Gias nodded. "We are running low, as we gathered in a hurry, but we will suffice."

"Very well. Lock yourselves in here again and only open if you hear three quick taps."

Elora headed for the bailey. She sucked in a breath at the sight of bodies lined-up and covered in linen. To Elora's relief, the garrison occupied the space, sorting the dead from the wounded. She spotted Mathias and ran to him. In all the chaos, it was wonderful to see someone with authority and order. Forgetting decorum, she embraced him.

He stiffened and stuttered. "My... my lady, it is a comfort to see you well. But what is wrong?"

She let out a sob. "I thought we'd lost the castle."

He shook his head, "No my lady, they never breached the walls, nor did they attempt to do so. All the fighting took place in the jousting arena, and, although many were wounded, we escaped to the safety of the fortress." He wiped his brow. "The attackers soon retreated. We are now attempting a census. We have sent for more troops from the capital to offer us reinforcements should another strike take place, but I hope this is all over."

"Most of the inhabitants are in the chapel. My uncle and cousin are in the cellars, and..." she hesitated, "the king is outside."

Mathias did a double take, and at the seriousness of her face, his eyes widened. "The k-king? King... Robert?"

"Yes, along with Owain and Gerard. They are waiting for us to signal their safety."

"Well then, let's open the gates!"

With Elora now gone, Gerard's heart hung heavy.

"She's the one your music is all about, isn't she?" The king laid a hand on his shoulder.

Gerard nodded, not taking his eyes from the castle.

"Now it makes sense. The bond between the two of you is strong."

He glanced at the king. "You see that? I'd wondered if I'd only imagined our connection, that what we shared was not real, rather the kind of love we sing about."

"Yes, love is confusing. We live in a world where we marry for a suitable match and security. Love is expressed between knights and maidens and written as poetry, but not expected to enter a marriage. I have been in love many more times than I'd care to admit."

"And Queen Arabella?"

"The love that exists between the queen and I goes deeper than mere attraction. We had an arranged marriage, but from the first moment I laid eyes on her, my breath was snatched from my body. I thought to myself, what had I done to be blessed with such a creature? But that is not the kind of love that I converse about."

Gerard thought back to the moment he'd seen Elora again, when his heart had skipped a beat at the sight of her. "It's not?"

The king shook his head. "No, my friend. A beautiful woman can turn many a man's head, but that is not love. Love is a choice—when we choose to love a person despite our current troubles. When I married Queen Arabella, I made that choice. I know that the concept of fidelity is not always practiced by the nobility. 'Tis thought that when we marry, not for love, but for convenience, that we must find happiness outside of marriage. But the day I took Arabella's hand, I made the decision to choose her, every time. And, if occasionally, I find my eyes wandering, my head reminds me of this. Such a covenant, when made between two people, is the kind of love that runs deep."

"'Tis what makes you and the queen so strong," Gerard whispered, almost to himself.

"Well, let us hope such love is as profound as I believe it to be. Or else we may encounter trouble when Arabella arrives and sees me after so many years."

They both shared a laughter that brought a tear to his eye. And then Gerard's thoughts turned once more to Elora. "But Lorie and I, we never made such a mutual choice. Can unrequited love run so deep?"

Robert twitched the whiskers growing around his chin.

"What makes you believe she does not return your love? Unacknowledged love is not the same as the absence of it. A woman's heart is complex. Who can begin to understand it? I wonder if the Lady Elora knows herself. Time, patience, and faith will go a long way."

"Time, we've had plenty of. Patience, I confess to growing less of recently. And faith?" He considered it for a moment. "That I could probably exercise a little more."

"Ah." King Robert chuckled. "Then return to your prayers, my good man. For the Holy Scriptures commands it, does it not? To pray without ceasing?"

The king was right. At what point had he given up hope for Elora? The moment she'd rejected him? Such time had passed. Mayhap if he'd spent the past few years praying rather than running, he would be in a better position. Still, here he stood, near the woman he loved. Perchance God had played a bigger part in this than Gerard had initially given him credit for. Was there still hope?

The wave of a white flag from the gatehouse towers caught his eye. "Highness... did you see that?"

They stepped out from the tree line as the gates to Carisleau Castle opened. "Could it be a trap, do you think? We've not seen any signal yet to say otherwise?"

To Gerard's relief, Elora appeared outside the entrance, next to Mathias. He sighed. All was well.

Chapter Eight

Elora watched Queen Arabella's entourage journey along the Morgandy Road leading up to the castle. Behind her, Lady Beatrice and Lord Reginald warmed themselves by the fire.

"How did this happen?" Uncle Reginald rubbed his hands together.

"It was a peasant uprising," said Elora, not taking her eyes off the distant path.

Aunt Beatrice snorted. "They certainly attacked us when we were least expecting them. With so many people in attendance whom we did not know, the jousting tournament provided a perfect time to attack."

Elora tore her gaze away from the outside and focused on her aunt and uncle. With their advancing years, Uncle's increasing blindness and Aunt's re-occurring headaches, she could hardly blame them for wishing to retreat to the fortified tower. "Has the king been made aware of the queen's arrival? It will not be long before she reaches our gates."

Aunt Beatrice glanced up but showed no effort at moving herself. "I do not know, dear. Would you be so kind as to..."

"Yes, of course." She planted a kiss on her uncle's forehead then her aunt's cheek. She hurried down the steps. Fresh white linens, decorated with boughs of summer evergreens, adorned the assembled trestle tables in the Great Hall. Their fragrance filled the place and calmed her nerves. Elora strode over clean floor rushes, and as the candles flickered, she cut a glance toward the musicians' balcony overhead. No one there. But music was the least of her concern now. As the queen's arrival grew imminent, she had to check on the king. He now occupied their finest chambers, and servants rushed to prepare him a bath and supply him with some of her uncle's best clothes. Soldiers guarding his entrance let Elora through.

She drew in a breath as she entered the king's solar, her heart beating so rapidly she had to cling to the sleeves of her dress. Ridiculous. He was the same man she'd been with in the forest only earlier in the day, and yet somehow, now that he'd bathed and shaved and was adorned in fine linen, he oozed regal authority.

"Highness." She bowed her knee.

"Please rise, my dear. Do you have news?"

She hitched her hem to stand as gracefully as her trembling legs would allow. "Yes, the queen nears. I can take you to greet her, if it pleases you."

She glanced his way and caught what seemed like uncertainty in his eyes. "Highness?"

He stared at his reflection in the looking glass and tweaked his mustache. "Will she think me much changed?"

Elora hesitated. Did he truly ask if she thought his wife, who'd not seen him in who knew how many years, would still find him handsome? What did he expect her to say about that?

"For the better, undoubtedly."

His laugh at her response came from deep within. "A diplomatic answer." He touched the scar beneath his eye. "They say our scars tell our stories... the trouble is, I'm not sure I want my stories to be told."

"You think they reflect the horror you endured in the war?"

He nodded.

"Perspective is everything, is it not? One person may see the trauma experienced, another, the tragedy overcome. I suspect the one who professes to love another would choose to view the latter."

King Robert turned from his reflection and tilted his head. "And you? Which view do you take?"

"I-I hope that I see things as Christ does, seeing past the superficial and straight to the heart."

"Ah yes, I remember Gerard mentioning that you considered taking the veil."

She blinked at the king's candor. Gerard had mentioned her? "I became a novice for a time... only I could not decide if it was the life for me."

"You returned home until you felt ready to take the vow?"

"Precisely."

He took her arm within his own. They proceeded along the cloisters and through to the bailey. "The question remains, which vow scares you the most?"

His query both alarmed and confused her, but the trumpets sounded once more, and the castle gate opened, stealing any time for clarification. The royal carriage, painted gold and white, rolled through into the courtyard, and the deep blue curtains moved gradually back.

Silence lingered as a foot appeared out of the carriage. The most sumptuous of dark red fabric came next, and then the queen, her small physique lost in an array of grandeur. She exited cautiously, helped by two servants. Tentatively, her head raised and her gaze locked with the king's.

Gerard witnessed the exchange between Robert and Arabella with interest. Would Arabella be glad to see Robert? Or be angry at his prolonged absence?

Queen Arabella hesitated, her eyes wide and glistening. Slowly, she moved toward Robert, reached out a hand to his hair, touched his face, then squealed and flung her arms around him.

Gerard looked away, giving them the privacy they deserved. Yes, their love ran deep. It stood the test of time, and no matter what had transpired between them, they still belonged together. The scene immediately inspired him to write another song. Mayhap he would. He flexed his hand muscles, not sure he'd be able to play again without discomfort. Perchance he'd been overly cautious.

Gerard headed to the Great Hall, settled himself down in the musicians' balcony, and plucked away on his lute. He soon found a melody line and rhythm to scribble on his parchment. Then the words flowed, and he wrote them on a separate page, singing them as he scribed, lost in the world of composition and music. He became vaguely aware of others in the room, but he did not stop for a moment, zoning out until the song had left him. He sat back and exhaled, blinking himself alert to the surrounding people.

He turned, finding himself face to face with Lorie. Her features held no clue to her feelings or thoughts. She picked the sheet up and looked at his notation. He again played the music that he had just composed. Before long, Elora joined in. Her harmony, so unique in its placement, sent shivers down his back. How could she question their destiny together? In moments such as these, no two hearts were so in tune. And after they had finished, a rapturous applause surrounded the room.

They turned round to face the source, and Elora's face inflamed.

"Huzzah!" The king clapped even louder. "You must

perform for us tonight, the both of you, together. Never have I heard quite so heavenly music and perfect musicianship between two people. Is it not so, my dear?"

The queen nodded vehemently. "Yes, my love, we must hear more. But giving so little time is not fair to them. After the melee tomorrow, would they do us the honor?"

Gerard bowed. "Yes, of course, it will be our pleasure." He daren't look to Elora for her confirmation. Indeed, he could sense her discomfort. Finally, he turned to face her, but she had disappeared as silently as she came. In her place were his band of minstrels, ready to do his bidding.

The king clapped his hands, signaling more music. Gerard sighed. He told the minstrels the mode and to follow his lead. He picked up his lute and played a vibrant tune, the joyous music drowning out the nagging feeling suppressed as he scanned the crowd of people. Plenty of food and wine had been brought out from the cellars to celebrate the king's return and the queen's arrival, and indeed the people were in a jovial mood, despite the tragedy of the day before.

He glimpsed Elora wind her way through the crowds. She headed for the door, but someone stopped her. He expected to see Aimee asking her to stay, but no, it was a man. With back turned, he had his hand protectively behind Elora. Who was this person?

Elora nodded and returned to the room. As the man coerced her back in, they took position in the center, bowed, and joined the others. As they danced, he spotted the fellow able to keep her from running. Mathias? This man clearly had eyes upon her. Did she have eyes upon him? Whatever it was between them, Gerard didn't like it.

The heat of the room and the closeness of dancing bodies proved suffocating. As she spun around the hall, left then right, Elora tried to keep the elegance that the music demanded, but her legs threatened to buckle.

Concern crossed Mathias's face. "You are not well. Let us get some fresh air."

Grateful for the change of scenery, she took Mathias's arm and allowed him to escort her outside. The crisp night air blew against her skin, and she exhaled in relief. As they reached the bailey, they met Morgandy soldiers returning from their scout of the area.

Mathias hailed them. "What news?"

"We've scoured the villages. No signs of any unrest amongst the peasants, and we have not found Aidan."

Elora let go of Mathias's arm and turned to face him. "What can be done about Sir Aidan?"

He furrowed his brow. "Well, if they believe he is the king, they will send demands for a ransom. We will simply have to bide our time."

"And if they discover his true identity? What then?"

Mathias sighed and glanced at her. "Let us hope they release him."

It had been a long day. She left Mathias to deal with the soldiers and headed for her chamber on the upper floor of the keep. She grimaced as her wounded leg throbbed, and she stopped midway to examine it.

"Elora."

She turned around, just as an out-of-breath Gerard chased her up the steps.

"Aren't you needed?"

"No, I'll not be playing anymore tonight, seeing as tomorrow we'll be..."

At the reminder of Gerard's commitment, she folded her arms.

"Lorie, I know you dislike performing, but you had already agreed to perform with me only days ago, and we could not turn down the king and queen."

"You think I'm cross with you because I have to perform?"

He hesitated. "Yes?"

She exhaled through pursed lips. She did not wish to fight with him. "I am not angry, Gerard."

He stepped closer and gazed into her eyes expectantly.

"Just... saddened."

He narrowed his eyes on hers. "I'm not sure I follow..."

"You answered for me, as if I wasn't even there. Completely invisible, with no voice at all. You didn't look at me or seek my opinion. We never used to do that. I loved how you included me as your equal, despite society's views on the matter. We approached life together, like in our music."

"Loved... you said loved. Not anymore?"

"You are missing the point, Gerard."

"You've just admitted that you once loved me. That is news to me. I'd thought you rejected my proposal because you didn't love me."

"'Tis not true, and you know it. I did not accept your proposal because I said I loved God more. That I believed he was calling me to take the vow, and if you loved me at all, you would let me go."

He flayed his hands. "And I did. I honored your request. I left for Morgandy and did not look back. So, what happened? You lied to me, is that it? God was your excuse, so that you didn't have to wound my pride?"

She gasped at his insolence. "What nonsense. Why are you making this all about you?"

His eyes became wide and his mouth opened, but she didn't want to hear his excuse. She thrust her fists against her hips. "I was sixteen, young and confused. An orphan. The only real mother I knew was Madame Evangeline, but she was not there to give advice. When we fell in love, my aunt led me to believe that it would pass, so I went back to the nunnery. But the longer we were apart, my desire for you only grew stronger. I returned to Carisleau the following year to tell you. Only to find that you'd left. Then I waited, and waited, but you never came back. The last I heard, you'd gone to war."

She took a step forward and peered into his eyes. "You always detested violence of any kind. And now, years have passed, and you've changed, and I've changed."

"Has your love for me ceased too?"

She sighed. "Love is not enough. After this week is over, you'll be moving on. You do not have a home but drift from place to place. And what would I be? What about children?"

His jaw tightened. "It's Mathias, isn't it? He has won your heart. I've seen the two of you together. He can scarce keep his eyes off you."

"Mathias?" Did he honestly think...? "He is a kind and respectable man, and I trust him implicitly. Indeed, I have reason to. Mathias has served my aunt and uncle faithfully for many years. But if you infer that there is any kind of romance, then my goodness... You were never the jealous kind, Gerard. This does not look good on you."

At her raised voice, she suddenly grew silent. She stepped back, embarrassed by her own boldness. "I am sorry. I do not wish to disrespect you." She forced a smile. "It has been a long day and I must go to my chamber."

"Wait—don't leave."

Gerard pulled her close, tilted her chin, and kissed her tenderly. She breathed in his scent of sandalwood and it awakened memories of the days spent together in the meadows of Carisleau.

"Do you love me?" His question came out hoarse with emotion.

She gasped as he let her go, and she touched her lips. The

words formed in her head, but somehow she couldn't bring herself to express them. And it panicked her beyond anything she'd known. Why couldn't she say it? She felt it.

Instead of confronting her feelings head on, her feet turned the other way, and she darted to the safety of her chamber.

Clarice jolted at her mistress's sudden arrival. "My lady? Is everything well?"

Elora's lip trembled. "I am in pain."

"Oh, of course. Let us tend to your wound, shall we?"

Elora welcomed the assistance as Clarice guided her toward the fire. The small action was comforting. Elora grimaced as Clarice removed the old bandage and applied fresh anointment to her wound.

A tear slid down Clarice's cheek. "My lady, I am to blame for the uprising. It is all my fault. Will you ever forgive me?"

Elora's eyes widened. Gracious, what had come over her maid? "My dear, I seriously doubt—"

"I am indeed. I may not have planned such an attack, but I knew one was coming only I chose not to tell you... my father—"

The door slammed open, and Clarice dropped her supplies in a fluster. A gush of wind entered along with her aunt, blowing out the candle that rested on the table. Recognizing Aunt Beatrice's demeanor, Elora tapped her maid's hand. "You may leave us," she whispered.

She sensed Beatrice's cold stare and, unable to bring herself to face her aunt's profile, cast her eyes to the ground. After Clarice left, Elora inhaled and braced for whatever was about to come. She flickered her gaze up. Aunt Beatrice stood by the doorway with her hands on her hips.

"You know why I am here."

Elora blinked. "I can assure you, I do not."

Wrong answer. Her aunt's lips thinned with apparent disdain.

"Truly? Are you so unaware? Did you not think others could see you on the stairs?"

Heat rose to her face. Her aunt saw the kiss with Gerard? "'Tis not what you think."

Beatrice's eyebrows arched. "No?" She shook her head, and stepped further into the chamber, her flurry of silk skirts swishing as she moved. "It appears we are here once again, returning to an old conversation."

Chapter Nine

The final day of the tournament arrived, finishing with the grand melee finale. Drums rolled, building anticipation for the event. The wooden stalls vibrated, and Gerard tightened the grip on his sword. "What can be gained by the king making his presence public?" he muttered under his breath.

Owain worked out the kinks in his neck. "Rest easy, friend. Word has already spread about the king's return, and it is fool-hardy to pretend otherwise. We've extra troops from Morgandy, and we're on high alert. If the peasants do indeed plan to revolt again, we are ready."

Gerard expelled a frustrated breath. "Mayhap you are right. Although I am surprised at such a vast turn-out. Why anyone would wish to return to the place that only days before had turned into a battlefield, is beyond me." And yet, the repaired pavilions held hundreds of spectators. If anything, more people had come, no doubt to witness for themselves the return of King Robert.

"It sends a clear message to the people, I'll warrant, that the king remains undefeated." Owain rose.

Gerard had to agree. The people were indeed in high spirits as they flung flowers to show their support.

Once the melee began, the clash of swords drew his attention. It conjured up an awful reminder of warfare, and he ground his teeth. He would not be caught off-guard again. His eyes scanned the landscape, noting key people's whereabouts. Satisfied all appeared well, he took his place beside Lord Reginald and Lady Beatrice. Elora sat on the bench opposite, her face appearing unusually stern. She stared ahead, her back straight and tense. He thought about moving over to her but caught the piercing glare of Lady Beatrice. What caused this tension here? Elora would not look at him—was she afraid to?

His eyes returned to the mock battle between the two teams, one fighting for Carisleau and the other for Morgandy. Both sides fought with veracity.

Gerard rolled his eyes at Owain's fidgeting. "You surely do not wish you were down there?"

"I do, and I'd do a better job too. Curse this stupid injury."

"Oh, I'm sure your prize will be worth it in the end."

"Why? Did you hear something?"

Gerard leaned forward and lowered his voice. "I believe Lady Aimee will reward the jousting champion at the closing ceremony."

"But I did not win."

"Aidan is not here to claim his award, so you win by default."

He snorted. "No man wishes to be second choice."

Gerard nodded. "Now that I can identify with." Logging the thought in his memory for a future song, he spotted a rider coming in on the Morgandy Road. He sat straighter. "Are we expecting a messenger?"

Owain shrugged. "Since when do we expect anything?" He squinted his eyes. "But that is not... the man is stooping over." The horse was running, but in no particular direction. "He's out of control. Is the rider dead?"

Elora paused in conversation with her uncle as Gerard and Owain left suddenly. Something about their demeanor gave warning. She followed them out of the royal box and toward the gatehouse. Mathias joined her. At the sight of the slumped figure in the horse's saddle, she slowed.

The body fell to the floor, and she gasped at his beaten state. Blood covered his head, hands, and feet. For what little clothing he had on, it did not extend to shoes. His eyes were swollen shut.

Gerard and Owain lifted him up. "Let's get him inside."

Elora ran behind them, lifting her dress so as not to trip on the hem. "But who is he?" She called after them.

"Aidan," said Mathias, as he fell in step beside her.

"King Robert's guard? The one who was captured?"

"I believe so."

"At least he is safe. But why did they spare him?"

"Mayhap they wished to deliver us a message."

They cleared a space for Aidan on a table in the infirmary. Gias tutted as he examined Aidan's broken body.

Gerard hovered nearby. "Will he live?"

Elora gently tapped Gerard's hand. "His injuries are severe, such beatings... we can fix what is on the outside, but we do not know what is happening inside. If you wish to converse with him, now might be the time to do it."

Gerard sucked in a breath. "We must fetch the king. He will want to speak with him."

"I'll go." Mathias turned to leave.

Elora flashed Mathias a grateful smile then squeezed her eyes shut in prayer before continuing to help Gias clean the blood away from Aidan's face.

"Aidan, we are here, good fellow." Gerard's tone was overly bright. "You are in the best of care."

Aidan tried to speak, but his injured throat prevented him. Elora pressed a linen to staunch the bleeding.

Gerard leaned in closer, and Aidan finally croaked out the words, "They attacked Morgandy... wished to gain control..." He coughed and spluttered further. "Forgive me, friend. I failed him."

"No, no you did not. You brought him safely home to us. You leave us with honor and glory, and your name shall live on."

"Put me in one of your songs... I'll be more famous than you." He managed a laugh then coughed again.

"Hush now and save your strength for the king is coming."

Aidan squeezed Gerard's hand, but then his breathing shallowed and stopped.

Elora whispered a prayer, then stepped back to give them some privacy, just as King Robert entered the chamber.

"What did he say?" He looked from Owain to Gerard, and to Gias. "Is he dead?"

"Yes, Highness. I am sorry for your loss. I know he was close to you." Gias closed the man's eyes, then folded his hands.

Robert broke down, weeping like Elora had never seen a man do. The scene became overwhelming, and she felt a sob rise in her own throat. Mathias placed a protective hand on the small of her back and guided her outside.

"My lady, you should be spared from seeing such things."

"I saw worse at the abbey."

"Then you are a strong woman indeed."

"My handmaiden said something to me last night about the uprising, but I was distracted and didn't act on her information. Could I have prevented this if I'd have spoken sooner?"

"There is little we could have done for Aidan, my lady. We would not have found him even if we'd ventured straight to Morgandy last eve. At least the queen is safer here than at the palace."

Elora nodded, thankful that they were all safe at Carisleau, but still, this certainly changed things. "What will happen now?" She looked up at Mathias, but noticed Gerard, his face grim and emotionless. Suddenly aware of the proximity between herself and Mathias, she took a step back.

"The king will send out scouts to determine what is happening in the capital, though I've no doubt he will raise an army and go to Morgandy's defense."

"Gracious, then I wonder about the melee—Uncle will surely wish to put it on hold. What do you think?"

"I fear it is too late, my lady. Once the men start fighting, there is little that can be done to cease warfare until one side is defeated."

Elora chewed the side of her lip. "But still, I must inform him. Thank you, Mathias." She scuttled back to the stalls as quickly and ladylike as possible. By the time she reached the royal box, her breath had escaped her. She glanced around until her eyes settled on Queen Arabella.

The older woman seemed to understand the magnitude and rose with regal poise.

"He is in the infirmary, Highness."

Queen Arabella's face bore a pinched expression, and she nodded in response.

"What is it?" Aunt Beatrice twisted to face them. "Is there trouble?"

"None to us, but the king's knight, the one that was captured... he is dead." Elora felt unshed tears sting her eyes.

Aunt Beatrice gasped and fanned her flushed face with a handkerchief. "Did this happen here?"

"I think not. It seems there is trouble in Morgandy. Uncle, do you think it wise to stop the melee? If King Robert should call the men to arms, it would surely be prudent to preserve our fighting soldiers as best we are able."

Aunt Beatrice tutted. "Do not be ridiculous. The melee is almost finished."

"Then what of the banquet? No one will surely be in good spirits to feast now."

"We will not cancel." Her aunt waved any such thought away with her hand. "After all, we are holding it in the queen's honor."

Uncle nodded his head. "Indeed, a feast and merriment are precisely what the folk here need to raise their spirits and take their minds off the outside troubles. We go on as planned."

Elora sucked in a breath and folded her arms into her abdomen. She sensed a stirring of trouble, but what could she do about it?

Clarice passed through the gates of Morgandy and glanced over her shoulder. Why did the capital of Edan's wall walk not house many soldiers? Pushing the thought aside, she continued down the cobbled streets, carefully avoiding the dirty stream of water in the center. She shivered, passing a gathering of rats eating the waste collecting by the buildings. She spotted a group of children lingering in the passageways between the shop rows, their thread-bare clothes hanging off skinny, dirty bodies. Circumstances were even more dire in the city than they were in Carisleau.

She went over to them and offered some bread. With wide eyes, they grabbed it from her and ripped into the food like a dog might devour its meat.

"Do you know where the rebels are meeting?"

The children simply shook their heads.

"I mean no harm. I'm looking for my father. I believe to find him amongst them."

The girl, the youngest of them all, mayhap only four or five years old, glanced up and pointed a bony finger toward the streets. "They're everywhere."

Clarice frowned and followed the direction in which the girl pointed. Shouts sounded from the market square. People ran and screamed. What could be happening?

Clarice picked up her pace, but the stampede of city dwellers came upon her.

She looked to the skies just as soldiers plummeted off the battlements. She gasped in disbelief. The uprising! They dared to seize control of the city? She spun round, taking stock of the situation. If she remained in the streets, she'd be trampled.

People fled to their homes. Shutters closed and the streets emptied. The city gates were sealed. Could she seek refuge in the castle?

The warning bell sounded as she sprinted up the hill, but the castle gates were already shut. The cathedral remained her only possible refuge. God help her. Why had she come? What had she possibly hoped to achieve here?

Clarice tripped and grazed her hands on the cobble. Muttering under her breath, she staggered toward the city's sanctuary along with others who fled for safety.

Chapter Ten

"There's an uprising in Morgandy."

Aimee, arm-deep in the gown chest, paused and looked up. Her face paled. "How do you know? Is it something to do with that soldier who died?"

Elora nodded. "I am afraid so." She glanced at Aimee pulling out dresses. "Where is Clarice?"

Aimee shrugged. "Said she had family matters to attend to. The poor girl seemed quite upset about something. I bid her leave. Why?"

"She said something to me last night about the uprising, and I wanted to question her about it. But if she's gone..." She sighed, saddened that she'd been too caught up with her aunt's intervention the night before to talk to Clarice. "I hope she is well."

Aimee nodded to a folded parchment sitting on the table. "A letter came for you."

Elora gasped, recognizing the seal. "It is from Riona." She longed read it, but she would wait until Aimee had been seen to. Picking up a comb from the dresser, she brushed Aimee's wild red curls, pinning them up and out of the way.

"So, what's happening with your Sir Gerard?"

"He does not belong to me, Cousin."

"Oh, does your heart know that?"

Changing the subject, Elora retrieved a pile of garments and lay them on the bed. "I must select a gown for tonight's feast. Should I wear red or gold do you think?"

"You ignore the question."

Elora let out a sigh. "He kissed me last night." As the words hit the empty air, her cheeks turned aflame.

"Did you kiss him back?"

"Of course not. I was so shocked that I departed for my chamber and locked the door behind me."

They burst into giggles.

"I'm not sure that was the best move." Aimee shook her head. "But you must follow your heart. That is all you can do."

Elora cast her eyes upward and flung her arms in the air. "Aunt says I am being selfish, that I am ruining your chances of a good match. Although I fail to understand how my alliance with Sir Gerard would affect you in any way."

Aimee chewed her lip. "She would say that if you wed a glorified minstrel, it would lower your social status, and have a direct impact on my own standing. She wants me to wed an earl or a baron, at least. A knight, even an esteemed troubadour knight such as Gerard, is not good enough for her. However, I do feel that is an excuse. After all, Father invited Sir Gerard here. He would not have done so if he did not want our family to be associated with him."

Elora sat on her bed and ran her fingers along the intricate beading of the claret silk. "Then what?"

"Mother has come to depend upon you. She does not want you to return to the abbey, even though it would be far more economical for you to do so. Neither does she wish you to wed a man that would not be advantageous to our family, for she would gain naught by it. Think on it, she does not have to shoulder the responsibility of running the estate because you are here to do it. And as long as she thinks you are beholden to her, you are an asset. Why did you reject Gerard in the first place?"

"Because Aunt convinced me that the marriage would be doomed to fail. That what I felt for Gerard was not love, but infatuation. I came to doubt my feelings, that they were sinful. Which was why I returned to the abbey. Only after I spent time with Madam Evangeline, did I come to doubt all that Aunt Beatrice had said."

"And now... how do you feel about Gerard?"

"When he is close to me and my heart starts thumping, and my knees buckle, well, that feeling of being so out of my depth—I cannot stand it."

Aimee patted her arm. "You speak of things I have little experience with. Though I've no doubt Riona will have an opinion on the matter. You said you confided in her in your recent letter, no?"

Elora glanced at the letter resting on the table. "Of course..." Breaking the seal, she unraveled the pages and sank into the sumptuous pillows that adorned the window seat.

My dearest Elora,

What a lovely surprise to receive your letter, indeed I am so excited to hear your news that I find I can scarcely write. I remember how heart-broken you were after making your decision to return to the abbey. And it sounds like the love you experienced all those years ago has not disappeared at all.

Of course, you've always loved the routine of the abbey, the rules, and traditions. Such things bring you comfort, I understand. But there is more, something better, something beautiful, and if you run toward it and give this a chance, I think you will be pleasantly surprised. And if you do decide to choose marriage, it is not being disloyal to God.

Granted, the apostle Paul said that it is better not to marry, and dedicate one's whole life to service, so no, I do not think it wrong if you choose to take the veil. However, the great apostle also instructed husbands to love their wives as Christ loved the church, and for wives to submit to their husbands. He chose not to wed, but he was not pushing that on everyone. We all have our paths to follow and our hearts to give. Make your own choice, not from your head, but from the depth of your soul.

I would love for us to meet again soon. My travels will not permit me time to come to Edan, but mayhap we could rendezvous in Salar? I will be visiting the Sisters of Mercy on my way back to Mairead. Why not consider visiting also? I have invited Cinnia and we could converse together as we once used to. I enclose the details of my journey.

All my love,

Riona.

Suddenly, the idea of returning to her childhood home and visiting Madam Evangeline seemed like a glimmer of light in the darkness. Elora clutched the piece of paper to her chest and leaned back against the stone wall. She would make mention of the idea to her aunt and uncle without delay. She finished dressing and made her way downstairs.

Quite remarkably, the queen's feast continued in the castle gardens, despite the day's earlier revelations. Gold and blue bunting hung from tree to tree, and candles in glass jars littered the landscape. The merry tune of the minstrels drew Elora's gaze to the wooden platform, but disappointment settled when she didn't see Gerard. Rumbles and whispers among the servants caused her anxiety to rise, and she glanced down at her dress self-consciously. What did they see wrong? No matter.

Elora picked up her pace and headed for the dais erected at the top of the garden. The queen perched there, but she noted the king's empty chair. Her aunt and uncle also appeared remarkably solemn.

"What is it?"

Aunt Beatrice nodded toward Queen Arabella, and upon closer inspection, Elora noticed the queen holding a letter in one hand and dabbing her eyes with her other. Arabella glanced up and forced a smile.

"The men are leaving."

Elora cast her gaze around the gardens and blinked at the absence of knights. A few men were here, but they were courtiers or servants—none of them fighting men. And this was the whole point of the banquet, to celebrate the knights' victories at the tournament.

"I see. They depart for Morgandy." Elora sighed with a nod of her head.

The queen's eyes widened. "You are most well informed."

"Does the king say what his plans are?"

"Only that they are journeying to Morgandy with an army to reclaim the city. A peasant's revolt, they suspect. I cannot help but feel the burden of such an outcome. The treasuries are bare. Taxes are high, and the common folk can't feed their children. Is it any wonder they have resorted to such measures to gain our attention?" Her voice quivered. "I am afraid that I am a terrible regent. This is my doing."

Elora gasped at Arabella's frankness. "My queen, you cannot shoulder this burden. I should have done more myself. Here I am adorned in gold and silk, and there are people outside the walls who are wondering where the next meal will come from."

Queen Arabella cast her gaze across the banquet of food. "And look at all this, a feast for men who are not here. What a waste."

"It does not have to be. Let us give the leftovers to the villagers. I doubt we will have much need of it, and yet it may go a long way in appeasing the unrest among the commoners."

Queen Arabella bore a pinched expression. "The food is not mine, but your uncle's."

Elora glanced across at her aunt and uncle.

"And I give it wholeheartedly, Highness." Uncle Reginald bowed. He waved his hands at the steward. "Please distribute the rest of this banquet amongst the poor, and let it be known it is given by the generosity of the king and queen."

Arabella leaned toward Elora. "Do you truly believe it will make a difference?"

"It is a start, my queen."

Such sadness enveloped her being, and she rubbed her arms, a slight chill coming over her despite the warmth of the mid-summer's night. Now was not the best time to discuss her departure. Deflated, she drifted toward a secluded spot in the garden and leaned over the stone wall which overlooked the road leading out to Morgandy.

"We've not a moment to lose."

Gerard packed his saddlebags and fastened the clasp on the back of his armor. "I'll be with you shortly, Highness. First, let me say farewell to our hosts—"

"No time, good man. Our very kingdom could be about to crumble. Now we have an advantage, for we at least know their location. But our element of surprise will not work if we arrive in broad daylight. Therefore, let us make haste."

He glanced up at the castle towers, where he knew Elora's private chamber to be. What would she think if he just departed like this, without so much as a goodbye? What if this spontaneous venture of the king's failed, and he never saw Elora again? If his kiss had been returned, mayhap he would find some comfort knowing that their love was mutual, but...

King Robert mounted his stallion. "Mathias, is your garrison sufficient to defend Carisleau in our absence?"

"Yes, my king. We have thirty men left to guard the towers and gatehouse."

"Then I leave the queen in your capable hands. I have sent word to her. I only pray she understands my actions in time."

Gerard blinked. Robert had not spoken directly to Arabella? When he planned for an element of surprise, he certainly held naught back.

But he would not leave without first speaking to Elora. He could not.

"Where are you off to?" whispered Owain.

"I'll not be long. Cover for me?"

"I think the king will notice if his favorite knight is not by his side."

"Then make an excuse. Come, man, you owe me as much."

Owain growled under his breath but gave a terse nod.

Sneaking through the crowds of knights readying themselves for the journey to Morgandy, he instead followed the sound of music round to the back of the castle where he knew the banquet would be taking place.

He spotted Elora at the dais, the summer's light catching her long golden hair, outlining her equally shimmering silk gown. Her appearance clearly turned several folks' heads, and she seemed none the wiser about how much of an impression she made. Oh, how he longed to stay with her.

He followed her at a distance, through the gardens, until she settled by the stone wall. She softly hummed the tune of the song they'd begun to write only a few days before, and without thought he completed the verse:

> *To leave and bid farewell*
> *I carry in my heart*
> *This song of ours of love be true*

E'en though I must depart

Elora spun round, and her eyes glistened. "Gerard!" She gasped and flung her arms around his neck. Forgetting propriety for one small moment, he drew her in closer, breathing in her scent of lilies. He kissed the top of her forehead and held her tightly. "I must leave."

"I know it."

He closed his eyes, pushing aside the dreaded feeling of history repeating itself. Unvoiced words clung to his lips, but he could not bring himself to say them. *Do you wish for me to return?* Over and over he said the words in his head, but the potential rejection he could not face.

As if answering his own heart, she pressed her forehead into his chest and whispered. "Please come back to me."

He placed a finger underneath her chin, and as she slowly gazed up at him, he saw the vulnerability and uncertainty in her eyes.

"After our kiss last night, and your frostiness toward me this morn, I thought..."

"I am sorry... 'twas not you I was upset with. My aunt had much to say on the matter, and I still have much to ponder on." She hesitated then shook her locks. "But the thought of you not returning is beyond contemplation."

Without further deliberation, he seized the moment, for there may never be another opportunity. As her lips met his, he savored their warmth, their tenderness. Finally, she pulled away, their hands still intertwined, and he released them with utter reluctance. "We will talk more when I return?"

"I shall hold you to that." She took a token from within her sleeve and passed it to him. The silk cloth had her initials sewn into the corner. "So that you will not forget me."

He laughed inwardly. "How long do you think I will be gone? I may well be back by the morrow."

Her eyes turned moist as a small smile curved her soft lips. "Until the morrow, then."

"Goodbye, my love."

He could not look back as he darted for the courtyard. The king's army had already departed, but they marched slowly along the road, so it did not take long for him to mount his horse and catch up to them. He slipped in subtly beside Owain as they journeyed toward the capital.

Their retinue comprised of the knights who'd competed, as well as the soldiers who'd accompanied the queen from Morgandy to Carisleau. A peculiar mixture of people, and not all were from Edan, for the tournament attracted knights from all over Caragh and beyond.

"How are your wounds?"

Owain shrugged. "If I stay absolutely still, I'm fine." He grimaced. "Trouble is, when the horse moves, I move. Fear not. I shall survive the fickle journey. It's whether I am fit to fight when we get there. Now that is the question."

"You and the rest of the knights, I should imagine. And this, after a week of tournaments. Who needs a melee to mark the end of the occasion, when we can have a rundown with the common folk? Mayhap we ought to order them in for next year's entertainment."

Owain winced. "Do not make me laugh, it hurts too much."

Gerard stifled a yawn. "I can't think of the last time I actually slept."

"Didn't you go to bed early last night?"

"Managed a few hours, but..."

"I see. You and Lady Elora have come to an understanding?"

"It is hopeful."

Owain nodded. "Then we must do all we can to get you back in one piece, hmm?"

Gerard and Owain picked up their pace and rode beside the

king at the front. As they settled into a rhythm, Gerard approached the king for details.

"They've seized control of the entire city, including the heavily fortified gates." Robert gazed ahead.

Gerard sighed. "And the castle?"

The king ground his teeth together. "I believe they are attempting to besiege it, although it remains ours for now. I've been a fool. The attack at Carisleau must have been a rouse to deplete my army and leave the capital unguarded."

Owain leaned forward in his saddle. "How many of them are there?"

Robert grazed a hand over his chin. "A few hundred, I am informed. We outnumber them, but they've secured the city wall and will let no one enter."

"I presume you have siege protocols in place?"

"Yes, the palace has a year's worth of supplies."

Memories of camping outside castles for years on end returned to Gerard. "This is a bold uprising. The majority of their troops are probably untrained, although they'll have some archers amongst them, I should think. If they infiltrate the castle they'll have claim to the entire kingdom. However, once inside the city, I doubt they will have many men on patrol. They may be under a false sense of security. We must strike quickly to reduce their size before they learn of our presence. Once under attack, your garrison within the castle will be there to protect us."

Robert shook his head. "But if we cannot penetrate the gatehouse, it does not matter how many men they have inside. I have summoned the barons' armies. We will regain control of Morgandy and avenge Aidan's death. No matter the cost."

After seven days spent trapped inside the cathedral with hundreds of other innocent bystanders, Clarice could take it no longer. Sickness and disease were beginning to sweep through the people of Morgandy and they'd ran out of food. She'd volunteered to venture out into the city to salvage further supplies.

She sucked in the air as it hit her face the moment she stepped out onto the streets. Floating ash fluttered in the sky like snow on a crisp winter's day. The small streets were littered with trodden food stuffs, human waste, and the dead—left untouched since the day of the invasion. The shops had been plundered. The city now lay in ruin. What hope had she of finding enough supplies for their folk?

Casting her gaze toward the castle, she noticed siege engines being built. Did they think that would be enough to infiltrate the most secure castle in the kingdom?

She decided to head to the gates. Mayhap she could return to Carisleau and seek help there.

At the sight of the heavily guarded gate, she gasped and hid behind a building. Was there no escape from this place? She scanned the men charged to guard the barbican. None of them looked like her father. She'd begun to wonder if he was here at all or if he'd perished.

Rubbing the goosebumps from her arms, she darted inside a tavern. Broken caskets of ale lay on the floor. No food or drink remained on these premises. But she noted the stairs and followed them up until she reached a small window in the roof. She climbed out to gain a better vantage point.

From here she could see beyond the city walls. The biggest army she'd ever seen marched toward her. Blue and gold banners fluttered in the wind, and soldiers lined the other side of the river. The king had come. Was there hope for them still?

CHAPTER ELEVEN

Naught had changed at the Sisters of Mercy. The nuns kept to the same routine, songs, and prayers.

Elora walked along the cloisters, as she used to do every day, and enjoyed the tranquility of the garden's fresh scent along with the quiet birdsong overhead. She passed by the infirmary and watched the nuns care for the sick, poor, and ailing. Then she ambled up the day stairs toward the dormitories and peered at the sparse furniture. She remembered the cold, scratchy blankets well—the one thing she'd not missed at all.

She continued on her memory tour to the library. Here, she'd learned to read, write, and illustrate. In an otherwise man's world, the nunnery gave her the opportunity to learn and discover, and despite its rigid rules and customs, it held a remarkable freedom that life as a lady in her uncle's castle did not.

Is that why she missed the abbey? She ran her fingers over the desk, touched the familiar powdered paints used for illustrations, and then walked through to the chapel. Remaining at the back, she listened to the sisters' singing. The purity in their voices reached up to the high ceilings and bounced off the stained-glass windows, surrounding her with heavenly music.

Madame Evangeline glided toward her, with arms resting within her sleeves. "My child, you have returned. Come walk with me."

They strolled outside, passed the lay sisters' quarters, and continued along the stream where the women collected water and washed their clothes. Elora smiled at the simplicity of life here.

"Did you come alone? Where is your handmaiden?"

Elora's thoughts flickered to Clarice, whom she presumed had escaped to Morgandy to find her family. She'd not mentioned her maid's disappearance to her aunt and uncle, who would no doubt take measures to punish the young girl for such a desertion. No, better for them to think she accompanied her now.

"One of my uncle's guards accompanied me. I also brought my cousin, but where she is, I have no idea. Aimee is no doubt exploring somewhere. I'm sure she will not be a bother to anyone."

"Not at all, dear one." Madame Evangeline smiled and cupped her face. "Your heart is conflicted."

Elora turned and studied Madame Evangeline's expression. "How could you know that?"

She took Elora's hands in her own. "Daughter, you were so very young when you came here. With no mother or father to care for you, we provided a haven and became your family. Your education has empowered you in ways other girls would dream about. We choose to consecrate our lives to God by refraining from marriage, but it does not mean that you should. You gave your heart to a young squire a long time ago, regardless of whether you know it. You are conflicted because you are trying to hold on to two worlds."

"Are you saying my fondness for the place of my childhood is wrong?"

"No, dear, but for you, it simply is that. A place of your

childhood. Does not the Bible state that a man shall leave his parents when he weds his wife? There comes a time when you must leave your childhood home and form your own new family."

Tears streamed down Elora's face. "But I have two homes. I feel that whatever decision I arrive at, I will be letting down people that I love."

"Your aunt."

She nodded. "My cousin feels that Aunt Beatrice wants me to remain at Carisleau, although she has never said as much to me."

"No, she would not, child, for your aunt is a proud woman, and does not want to be seen beholden to anyone. Still, there is clearly an affection for you there, even if she struggles to show it."

"Then what am I to do? I cannot marry Gerard without the blessing of my aunt and uncle."

"Have you spoken to your uncle about it?"

Elora paused. "No, indeed."

"Then that is a good place to start."

Elora toyed with the hem of her sleeve as her thoughts drifted to the king's armies at Morgandy. Would it not be ironic if she finally chose the man to marry then he died in battle?

"There is something else on your mind, is there not?"

Elora told her of Gerard's return, his commission as a troubadour, and how music had reunited them. She sighed. "But now I fear for Sir Gerard's safety."

"But I thought you said he'd returned from the campaigns."

"Have you not heard about the uprising in Morgandy? The peasants have taken control of the capital, and Sir Gerard is there with the king."

Madame Evangeline drew a heavy hand to her chest. "The king lives?"

"Yes. He was reunited with the queen at Carisleau, that is until the peasants attacked Morgandy in their absence."

"And they are evicting them by force?" She tutted under her breath. "Hungry folk do awful things when they are desperate. 'Tis unfortunate the king cannot show a little kindness rather than an iron fist."

"My sentiment also, and I conveyed my thoughts as much to the queen. However, how are they to even reason with the people if they cannot get through the gates? I doubt their leader is willing to parle with them."

"'Tis a shame their catapults cannot fling loaves of bread over the wall instead of fire balls."

"I think the time has passed to appease the uprising by a mere loaf of bread, Madame."

"Mayhap, but I believe, my dear, you must go there and be an influence."

Elora blinked. Had she heard Madame Evangeline correctly? What a preposterous notion. "They'd not let me enter the encampment, let alone get close to the king—"

"You are a daughter of the King of Kings. All things are possible with God. I will be praying for you, that the Lord God goes before you. You are His servant, are you not?"

"I am."

"Then heed His voice, and you must hasten, child, for I sense time is running out."

"But I am here to meet Riona and Cinnia. I surely cannot leave now. It took me several days to get here—"

"I gather Riona's arrival will be delayed, and Cinnia declined the invitation. You would be letting down no one."

Elora sighed, glancing around the place as if in a final good-bye. Indeed, it was a nice place to visit, but it was no longer her home. She need no more persuasion on the matter. Gerard may not be too happy to have her so close to danger, but she had been praying for God to speak to her about this… to do naught would be the worst kind of response.

"Then can I trouble you for some supplies?"

Madame Evangeline smiled. "Follow me. Then once you are on your way, I will head to Carisleau with a few of the others. We will explain things to your uncle."

"There is naught else for it, we must resort to fire." The king's tone held a tinge of sadness.

Gerard grimaced. How had it come to this? They'd been besieging the city walls for days, but they were too high, too thick.

"You'll burn down the city? What of the people inside, or the cost of rebuilding? This is your home."

"What else can be done? If I lose the capital, I lose everything."

"We could use smoke to disguise our next attack and continue with the battering ram."

The king sighed. "Our men are discouraged and tired. We need something more than smoke."

"And what if they've taken measures to resist fire? They could have thrown water on the roofs—"

"They're peasants, Gerard, not trained soldiers. I doubt they know the strategies of war like we do. Make it happen."

Robert's argument held merit. What else could they do? "If we wait a while longer, they'll run out of supplies. We have the advantage here." What had happened to the king's stamina since the campaigns? He'd run completely out of patience. "'Tis not your fault, you know, what happened to Aidan."

"Is it not?" The king's head snapped up. "He was taken because I was too cowardly to be myself. They took him, thinking him to be me, and then killed because he wasn't. You explain to me how I am not to blame." He sighed and straightened his spine. "And now my cowardice has killed hundreds more. No, I will not wait here any longer. I must breach the walls or I'll surely die trying."

Gerard bowed his head and departed from the king's tent. He strode through the rest of their encampment, inspecting the siege ladders being built and the repaired weaponry. Then he passed the tent housing the injured men and paused as a flutter of nerves ransacked the pit of his stomach. The female voice treating the wounded sounded remarkably familiar. He knew it was Elora before he'd even parted the canvas back.

"Elora? Why are you here?" He scoured the place for someone in charge, but found no such person.

She looked up, a flicker of surprise crossing her features, before she tightened the bandage around the man's arm.

"Helping, of course."

"What, you just found our camp and decided to help?"

She pulled a face. "No indeed. I came with my cousin. We offered our assistance." She washed her hands in a bowl of water, removed a soiled apron, and motioned for him to accompany her outside. "We only arrived this morning, although I note that my dear cousin has disappeared."

Gerard arched an eyebrow. "Yes, I do believe where there is work, Aimee is scarce. She has no doubt found herself more useful where there are more soldiers and less..." he waved his hand, motioning to the infirmary.

She flashed him a knowing smile then let him guide her out of the earshot of others. When they had found a secluded area by the trees, he took her hand and pulled her closer to himself. "You should not be here, Lorie. 'Tis not safe."

Her eyes widened. "And is it for you?"

"No, but I am resigned to the reality of my mission."

"And so am I. What is happening here? I had hoped you'd breached the walls by now."

"If only that were so. The king has plans to launch fire. We are building siege engines, but the king is growing impatient."

She gasped. "Fire will destroy Morgandy."

"It will."

"And the people."

He drew a sharp intake of breath. "That too."

"This cannot be so. They are commoners, Gerard. They're doing this to force change, do you not see? They wish to conquer a city no more than we do. They simply want a fairer system." She shook her head. "I thought the king had reconciled himself to that. Isn't this why he took so long to return to us, because he wished to find out the will of the people?"

"That is true, but the king is angered by what happened to Aidan. He is not thinking so clearly."

Elora sighed and sat on a rock, looking out across the water. "I love viewing the city from this vantage point. The wall so reminds me of Carisleau."

"It does?"

"It was engineered by the same architect, after all. Look, it has the same stone patterns." She pointed to the area where the flagstones formed a patterned arch. She stilled. "Praise be to God, it surely cannot be!"

"You've lost me now, Lorie."

"The wall... I think it has a sally port. There, don't you see?"

"The king would have mentioned it if he'd known about such a thing. No, this wall is fortified to keep people out. A sally port only weakens the defense."

She sat straighter. "Not necessarily. Ours is centuries old and disguised by the rest of the castle wall. It is not visible to others unless you know what to look for. I did not know about the sally port at Carisleau until Uncle showed me. Indeed, I assured him I'd never tell anyone about it, but if it can save a city... It surely cannot hurt to see."

"You are not going anywhere near that wall. You'll be shot

down in an instant." He hesitated and rubbed his beard. "But if a sally port exists, it changes our strategy immensely."

Keeping Elora close, he guided her through the encampment until they reached the king's elaborate blue and gold tent. The guards let them through, and they waited at the entrance until King Robert motioned them in.

Robert sat in his chair, his head tilted and resting on one of his hands. He straightened when he noticed Elora with Gerard.

"What is it? You bring me news?" He glanced from one to the other.

"Lady Elora has an idea, Highness. She believes it possible to enter the city walls through a hidden sally port built long ago."

King Robert chuckled, and it grew into deep laughter. He rose from his throne and paced the length of the tent, shaking his head.

Elora glanced back at Gerard. What had he been thinking, bringing her with him? The king could be a foreboding character. Gerard took her quivering hand and sent her a reassuring gaze.

"I have heard of these 'sally ports' that my predecessors built into their walls, but if they do exist, no one knows where they are. Do you not think, if I could locate such things, we would have exhausted the option a long time ago?"

Elora stepped forward. "May I?" She motioned to his writing desk, and upon his nod, she sketched a wall with markings around an arch. "This is the sally port that exists at Carisleau Castle, the secret entrance we used that night when we first met you in the woods. This part is movable and behind it is a small entry way. Our castle was built during the time of the Chaudors Dynasty. It stands to reason that the city wall, which they also erected during their time, would have a similar mechanism."

The king stopped pacing to eye Elora's sketch. He picked up the parchment with a quivering hand. "I dare not hold on to such hope, but if we could succeed in entering the gates at night..."

"Then we can attack them unawares."

"And regain control of the city."

"Then I pray God opens this door for us. Very well, we investigate it this night." King Robert rolled up the parchment. "But if this turns out to be naught, we strike with fire on the morrow."

The water was cold and dirty. Elora held back the urge to gag as she swam through the sewerage infested moat surrounding the castle. Gerard reached the wall first, then Ambrose and Owain. She glanced up at the stone in the near darkness, her heart thumping loudly, her breath more rapid with each intake. No ledge protruded on which to climb onto, and with the lack of light, there appeared to be no real way of discerning where a lever would be. She touched the wall, her hand cold and slippery as she fumbled about, feeling for the markings. "I-I can't find it," she whispered as her legs kicked wildly, trying to keep afloat.

Gerard motioned to the others, and together, they leaned upon each other forming a human ledge to support her weight. She seized the opportunity to climb out of the frigid moat. The wind chilled her wet skin, and her teeth started to chatter.

Heavenly Father, help me this night. An idea surfaced in her mind. Her uncle knew how to open the sally port, and he was blind. Follow the markings, he'd said.

Elora closed her eyes and rested her hands on the stone. She fumbled about until she felt a recess in the stonework. The engraving proved to be a line, pointing to another, and then another. She traced the line upward and around until it came to the shape of a star. And in the center of that star, she found a small circle. As her fingers followed, her hand discovered a slight hole in the rock. She gasped. "I've found something."

Men patrolled the wall walk above them, so she held her breath, waiting for them to pass. A few moments went by, and they continued to linger, however they were too busy talking, laughing, and drinking ale to pay the intruders any heed.

She reached down once more to the lever, but her damp and cold fingers slipped. As time wore on, the men grew tired, and her platform began to shake.

You can do this.

She pulled out her hand, wiped it on her wet clothing, and tried once more to budge the lever. It began to give way, and the sound of grinding penetrated the night.

"Let me." Gerard whispered.

Elora nodded and made room for him to give the stone a hefty push.

The sally port entrance appeared much smaller than the door at Carisleau, but large enough for them to climb through. Gerard went first, then Elora followed. They arrived in a quiet street near the church.

Gerard nodded to Owain and Ambrose. "Secure the wall walk. We'll head to the gatehouse."

Gerard grabbed Elora's hand. They ran along the edge of the city, keeping close to the dark wall, until they reached the barbican.

Elora hesitated. "I thought you were going to send me back."

"I considered it, but reasoned you'd be safer close to my side than out of my sight."

She almost smiled at the notion, but at the sound of more rebels, she froze. Gerard nudged her out of the way, then drew his sword upon the first before he could sound an alarm. The next few moments blurred as Gerard transformed from gentle troubadour into a warrior. She gasped as blood spilled, thankful that it was not her own, but sorrowful for the poor soul who'd lost their life.

"Elora, the gate! Open the gate!"

It took a while to shake herself from the numbness that had rooted her feet to the ground. Gerard had paved a clear path to the gatehouse, so she looked about haphazardly. What did she know of opening such a magnificent contraption? What could be done? She dare not shout out.

A sudden commotion came from above, and a body landed firmly next to her. She stifled a scream.

Relief replaced fear as Gerard, joined by Ambrose and Owain, darted forward. The portcullis opened. Its creaking sounded so loud, Elora felt certain they'd be discovered before they'd chance to besiege the city.

And then, a charging roar exploded, soon followed by a stampeding crowd of the king's mounted knights galloping through the city gates.

The sight quite took her breath away. A multitude of foot soldiers followed the horses. The rumble of marching reverberated, and like locusts swarming the city, the king's infantry infiltrated Morgandy. King Robert led from the front, his white horse standing on its hind legs. He lowered his arm, signaling the command for a fresh wave of warriors to sweep in, and take the usurpers by force.

"Save as many as you can," shouted Robert. "Take them to the towers to await trial."

Elora stood further back, wary of getting trampled in the commotion and watched helplessly as the king's men assumed control of the city

She'd played her part. Relief consumed her being as her body began to tremble. She rubbed her damp arms and fought back the tears, suddenly realizing how out of place she felt. What could she do now?

"Lorie." Gerard rode toward her. He scooped her up in one

swift movement. With a deep sigh, she snuggled up to his body, clinging to him as they galloped through the streets and away from the fighting. They returned to the encampment. Then he picked her from the saddle and carried her into his tent.

"Thank you," he muttered tenderly, his lips brushing her forehead. "The king owes this victory to you."

"I-I did naught but swim in a river and open a door."

He grazed his hand against her temple. "Little Lorie, ever the humble one." He pulled her into an embrace. "I must return now, but you get yourself warm and dry. Try to rest, if you can, for the real work will begin for you soon."

Gerard was right. They may have penetrated the gates, but there would be many more injuries to come before the night was out.

Chapter Twelve

Gray ash still lingered in the atmosphere several days after the conclusion of the besiege. Elora coughed into her arm as soot tickled her throat, and then she stilled as the Carisleau carriage arrived in the street. She'd been anticipating their arrival, but part of her had hoped this confrontation could be avoided.

Wiping dirty hands on the back of her dress, Elora braced herself as Uncle Reginald and Aunt Beatrice stepped down. She greeted them both and showed them inside the dilapidated building that she and Clarice had turned into an infirmary—one of several stations established all over the city. She had to contribute in whatever way she could. To return home so soon after the uprising deemed unthinkable. She would do whatever it took to convince her guardians of her required presence. Rolling up her sleeves, she followed them inside.

She motioned for them to sit at a table. Clarice served them bread and ale, freeing Elora to speak with them.

"How was your journey?"

"Long indeed." Aunt Beatrice wiped her brow. "Where is

Aimee? She sent a messenger asking for us to collect her, but now she is not even here to welcome us."

"Upstairs, getting ready. Won't you have some refreshment?" She motioned toward the food Clarice had set out.

Uncle Reginald rose from his chair. "Please excuse me. I will seek Aimee out. Clarice, will you lead the way?"

Clarice linked her arm through Reginald's and guided him out of the room, leaving only Elora and her aunt. Elora frowned. What could her aunt possibly have to say to her? She'd not spoken with Aunt Beatrice alone since that night when she'd scolded her for the 'kiss'.

Uneasy with the awkward silence that lingered between them, Elora initiated the conversation. "How have you been?"

"I believe my headaches have worsened."

Elora chewed the side of her mouth, biting back the frustration that began to surface. "Did Gias not give you his herbal remedy?"

"Elora, we did not travel all this way to speak of such trivialities."

"No indeed, you came for Aimee."

"We came for you both." Her aunt raised a finger. "It is high time you came home—'tis not safe for you to be inside the city. We thought you to be in Salar, and it came as quite a shock to receive Madame Evangeline's news. Really, Elora, I thought we'd brought you up better than this."

Elora cleared her throat. "Forgive me, Aunt, but you did not bring me up at all. The nuns did, and for this I have been trained to serve." She waved her hand around the makeshift infirmary. "You will be happy to know that Aimee objected to my desire in coming here, but she did not wish to abandon me, so you should be very proud of her. But you did not raise me. You sent me to the convent my entire childhood and, consequently, I have acquired different ideals. It should be of no surprise to you that I wish to help when there is trouble. But that is not why you are here, is it?"

At her aunt's stunned silence, Elora continued.

"You wished to speak frankly, then let us do so. You still harbor anger toward me because of Gerard. You know he is in the city. You came because you wish to put a stop to something from happening, just as you did all those years ago."

"You blame me for your refusing him?"

Elora's voice caught in her throat. "I do indeed. You told me I could on no accounts wed him."

"I did no such thing. I have no right to. I merely advised that to pursue wedlock with a man with no means of decent income and no home to call his own would not have been prudent."

Elora pushed back her chair and swirled round, turning her back to her aunt. To even gaze at her face caused her stomach to sicken. "I understand your reasoning then, which is why I heeded your counsel. But now, not only is he a man of good character but also of social standing. What objections could you possibly have to him?"

"None."

A small robin landed on the windowsill and chirped a cheery song, as if announcing something of great import to all those in the room. Then it fluttered away as quickly as it came. Oh, to be free to do what she pleased like that bird. Elora blinked at the almost comical interruption. Then her aunt's response settled in her mind.

"Pardon me?" She turned slowly, face to face with Aunt Beatrice. There was no malice in her eyes. If anything, did she detect a degree of remorse?

"Sir Gerard is a fine man, and a good friend of your uncle, a fact Lord Reginald is quick to remind me of." Her aunt sighed and angled her head. "I have been unfair to you. I see that now. I pushed for you to go to the abbey, and you obliged. I pushed for you to remain at Carisleau, and you did so willingly. I suppose that I have grown accustomed to your kind, accommodating nature, and did not want for things to change. I told myself that I had your best interest at heart, but I see now, I only had my own."

Elora's heart broke to witness her aunt's sincerity. Never had the woman been so open with her. "I thought you came here to take me home."

Beatrice rubbed her temples. "Yes, if you wish to return, but the choice is up to you."

Elora swallowed and inhaled deeply. "I wish to stay. At least for now. There is much work to be done, and I hope to—"

Aunt Beatrice nodded. "I understand, and this time, I will not interfere. You are your own woman. Clarice will stay with you until you are ready to come back."

For the first time in a long time, the heavy burden, which Elora had been unaware she even carried, lifted. Like the robin, she had the freedom to choose. But did it come too late?

"I do not know how I would have survived these past few weeks if you'd not been here, Clarice. Uncle would not have permitted me staying here without you by my side."

Clarice dipped her head, pink tinging her cheeks. "I should never have left Carisleau in the first place. But at least, despite my poor choices, good came out of it in the end, and we managed to find each other."

"Indeed, 'twas a miracle. What is to come of your father since his capture?"

She glanced at the floor. "I could find out very little from the jailhouse. Only that he awaits trial."

"Oh, I'm so sorry."

Clarice nodded. "He would not listen to reason, so he must face the punishment that he is given. It's my family I am fearful for the most. My mother is left alone to work the land in order to feed my brothers and sisters."

"Mayhap we can find her work at Carisleau. I am sure they could use another laundry maid. Besides, I have heard the king intends on reforming the system, and I am hopeful that he will release the prisoners. Mayhap your father will be back soon if he shows remorse."

"I can only hope and pray." Clarice stared at the tiny parchment that Elora toyed with in her hands. "What is that you constantly carry?"

"A song I've been working on. A song for Gerard."

"I know you are shy, m'lady, but words pour from your heart and onto the page. Mayhap this is the way you can show him how you truly feel."

"He knows how I feel. That is just it. He promised to return to me, so that we could talk. But he—"

Elora waited for the approaching tavern wench to serve them and folded her arms. She'd planned it in her head. After the mighty victory at Morgandy, she'd pour out her heart to Gerard and ask his forgiveness. Only Gerard had been recruited by the king to remain in the palace, and even though she too had stayed in the city to help with the wounded, their duties in the chaos prevented their contact. But order had been restored. She would soon need to venture home.

Elora paid the woman. "It's quiet in here today."

"Have you not heard? The king is holding a banquet this night. He even has the grand Gerard de Castille performing. That's where most folk are, I expect."

The shock of hearing Gerard's name mentioned caused Elora to pause her munching. With a mouth full of bread, she sputtered and swallowed. "He-he is? 'Tis the first I've heard of it. How do you know—"

"The town crier came through earlier. Said something about a banquet tonight, and he would be performing."

Elora looked at Clarice. "Is it open to all? This banquet? I know not how we missed the herald." She tutted to herself in rebuke.

Clarice gripped Elora's shoulders and looked at her square in the face. "Go to him."

"But it is simply not done for women to go chasing knights around the city."

"It is now or never, I'd say. How can you sit here, knowing how close by he is? 'Tis is only a short walk to the castle."

She held back the tears as her eyes glanced over the rolled-up scroll. How could he know how she truly felt if she'd not pluck up the courage to tell him so? "Very well."

Clarice's voice grew high in excitement as she pushed back the chair. "Then we've no time to lose." She grabbed Elora's arm and dragged her out of the booth.

"But what about your food?"

"Never mind that. We can eat later."

Her lungs burned as they sped up the steep hill toward the grand castle, its gleaming whitewashed walls drawing them closer. The castle gates hung wide open, so they followed the crowds through to the bailey. A large dais stood proudly in the center, and an array of musicians dressed in fine burgundy sat poised upon the stage.

A flutter of nerves began to surface as Elora pushed through the horde. She'd not seen anything so big, so extravagant. She breathed in the opulent scent of perfume that clung to the summer night air. Candles flickered everywhere, rich red and purple fabrics adorned the stage backdrop, and gold decorations glistened.

Then she spotted Gerard. Now was not the time. In front of all these people. No, she would wait until after the performance...

But then he turned to her and he froze. Their eyes locked, and there was no going back.

Gerard lay down his lute and paused, transfixed by the sudden appearance of Elora. Her silk red dress shimmered in the candlelight, the perfect picture of a rose, and her long flaxen hair cascaded down her shoulders like a veil.

He was so shocked to see her standing here, in front of everyone... drawing attention to herself. The thing she desired the least. Yet, he could not pass up such a rare opportunity, and without thinking, leaned into the crowd and held out his hand to her.

She came forward a little reluctantly but did not resist as much as he'd anticipated.

King Robert clapped his hands. "Splendid! Are we not promised a performance from this fine couple, my dear?"

"Indeed, Gerard, you did not mention she would join us today."

Gerard swallowed, his voice lost. "Ah, it is a surprise, Highnesses"

"Wonderful, well, we look forward to hearing your music."

Gerard motioned to the other troubadours to play, giving him and Elora a moment's privacy before they would undoubtedly have to perform something together. Noticing every eye still upon them, he took Elora's hand and stepped behind the platform curtain, thankful the music would drown out their voices from any quizzical onlooker.

Finally alone, he held Elora's fingers and drew her close. His heart pulsated rapidly, as he tried to gauge Elora's motive for being here. Her face appeared flushed, and her eyes wide.

She cast her gaze to the floor. "I am sorry. I should not have come. Only I was desperate to speak with you... I thought you might seek me out..."

"I've yet been unable to return to Carisleau."

She shook her head. "Carisleau? No, I've been here all this time in the capital. You did not know?"

Why had he assumed Elora would venture home after the battle? Of course, it would have been in her nature to help in any way she could. She'd been here all along? He'd been a fool.

"I've had ample time now, you see, to do a lot of soul searching. It has become so clear to me..."

Someone clearing their throat reminded him of their commission.

"We must perform together, but what shall we do? Do you think you can remember *Love's Creed*, or how about *Meadow Weeps?*"

"Let us sing our song from the fayre. I've written another verse. Do you remember it?"

"Yes, yes, I do, in fact." He rifled through a pile and retrieved a piece of paper covered in scribbles and further annotations. He smiled sheepishly. "I've been working on it, too. We can add another verse if it follows the same rhythm and tune?"

"Mm hmm, it does indeed." She nodded. "Shall I begin as we did before?"

"Yes, you start and finish, and I'll follow you. This is your song, after all."

They took their positions on the stage, Gerard strummed on his lute, and then nodded for Elora to begin. Her voice, gentle yet strong, reached notes higher than a lark's. And as they had done so that day at the fayre, he sang an alternative song above her own. Their harmonies collided in a musical cacophony, forming a new sound, a blend unique to their own connection. He dropped out, leaving Elora to take the last verse alone.

My heart blooms with love
And sings as thee draw near.
Please accept this red rose
I give my love to thee.

As she finished, silence lingered momentarily before an eruptive applause drowned out the sound of his beating heart. The faces surrounding them turned into a blur. He took Elora's hand and held it to his lips.

"I would love to wed you, Sir Gerard de Castille, with all my heart."

He hushed her with his finger on her lips. "You finally accept my proposal?"

Her eyes glistened, and she smiled at him. "If it still stands."

Overcome with joy, he picked her up and spun her round.

"Good men and women, we are betrothed!"

Cheers roared through the bailey.

She took his hand in hers and tugged him down to hear. "Do you not need to first ask my uncle?"

He shook his head. "Lord Reginald gave his consent weeks ago."

Her eyes widened. "He did?" She wondered if her aunt knew. Mayhap that was another reason for her visit earlier. She sighed and angled her head at Gerard's stack of music. "What else have you got here?"

He shrugged. "Plenty of new songs. If only I knew somebody who could read music..."

She picked up the harp and settled in a spot next to him. "Good that you have me then."

His heart swelled with love for this woman. God had heard his prayer.

Epilogue

Their wedding took place at St Winifred's Abbey, a short walk away from their new home granted by King Robert for their service to the crown. Elora particularly liked its location just outside the city, as from here she could help the church dispense alms to the poor, a mission field much encouraged by Madame Evangeline.

The king also asked them to continue Master Jacques Lonrique's work, because of his advancing years, and so Gerard and Elora remained in Morgandy to pursue music together.

"You are a sight to behold," said Gerard, as they stood outside their new home. She looked up at him and brushed away a wisp of his chestnut hair, its natural wave framing his square jawline. She tugged fondly at the dimple in his chin, and she kissed it.

He drew her into an embrace and held her so tight, she could feel his heartbeat.

"I love you, Sir Gerard de Castille, and I plan on telling you every day."

"Oh, my little Lorie, what did I do to deserve you?"

"Less of the little please. I'm tall for a maiden, and you know it." She took his hand and they walked along the path leading up to their house. Flowers bloomed around the door, and ivy grew up the walls.

"'Tis not as grand as Carisleau Castle. Will you be content here, do you think, away from your family?"

Elora's thoughts turned to Aimee, who remained very much unwed and showed no sign of settling on a suitor any time soon. She'd wondered if she and Owain would form an attachment, but no such thing had occurred, and the rest of Gerard's men had continued on the knight's circuit. "I do feel a little guilty for leaving them. Who will tend to Aunt Beatrice when she has one of her turns?"

Gerard scooped her up into his arms and carried her over the threshold, kissed her tenderly, and shut the door behind them. "They have a castle full of people, servants, and nobles alike. Not to mention your cousin. It is time she stepped up and took some responsibility herself. If leaving them is all that troubles you, then worry not, my love. My concern is that you may have left the finer things in life for a simpler way of living."

He set her down. She perused the vast rooms with simple but comfortable furniture. The kitchen seemed adequately large, and the sitting area nice and cozy. She continued through the house in silence, her footsteps reverberating around the room. She reentered the hallway and grinned. "Listen to that."

Gerard cocked an ear to one side, paused, and then shrugged. "I hear naught."

Elora smiled, a deep, contented smile. "Precisely. Peace and quiet, just as I like it."

"That is until the place is overrun with all the children we'll no doubt have."

"Why Gerard de Castille, we've scarce been wed a day!"

He grinned and pulled her closer. "Shall we investigate the rest of the house? There is another floor..."

She nestled her hand within his and followed him to the hall. "Ah, this shall be our music room, I think."

"Or a library."

"The possibilities are endless." She spun round to catch his gaze. "Yes, I think we shall be very happy here, my love."

And he responded with another kiss.

About the Author

Rachel has an MA in Creative Writing and loves to write fiction that uplifts, inspires, and encourages others. She lives in Yorkshire with her husband and three adorable girls, and when not writing she enjoys idling time away in a vintage teashop or visiting a historic landmark in pursuit of a new story!

To stay updated with Rachel's upcoming releases and giveaways, you can subscribe to her newsletter at **rachelajames.com/newsletter** and receive a free ebook.

Discover more about Rachel at: **rachelajames.com**